Birth of an American Gigolo

Published by Tenacious Books

Published in 2016 by Tenacious Books
Deek@DeekRhewBooks.com

Cover Design
Anita B. Caroll
Race-Point
www.race-point.com

Interior Design
Ellie Sipila
Move to the Write
www.movetothewrite.com

Content Edits
Anya Kagan
Touchstone Editing
www.touchstone-editing.com

Content and Line Edits
Erin Rhew
Tenacious Books
www.ErinRhewBooks.com

www.DeekRhewBooks.com

Birth of an American Gigolo

Deek Rhew

"Attraction begins with the eyes and the body. But seduction begins with words. Charm the mind, and the body will follow."

Henry S. Alabaster
Love, Life, and Other Bric-a-brac

Part 1

Chapter 1

Lindsey's nose hairs curled as odor from the bag on the floor assaulted her. She pushed the brown paper sack away with her foot, but the aroma still besieged her, encircling her head like rabid biplanes taking down a giant gorilla before it destroyed New York City. The little waiting room provided no alcove to escape the stench and no window from which to throw it.

Laughter echoed from behind the closed conference room door, and she drummed her fingers against her crossed arms. If she could have shot laser beams from her eyes, she would have singed the inhabitants.

The voices drew nearer, and her husband, Stewart, emerged from the entrance, though his attention remained absorbed by someone behind him. "Thanks for taking care of that, Cindie." He pointed his finger like a gun and dropped the thumb-hammer. "Pa-pow! You're the best!"

A shrill little laugh replied, "Anything for you, Stewie."

Lindsey ground her teeth together until her jaw ached and her temples threatened to split open like the San Andreas Fault.

Stewart halted mid-stride, breathed in deep through his nose, and rolled his eyes. Inhaling the stench should have sent him into a spastic seizure. He smiled a goofy, lopsided grin. "Smells so good." His I-just-had-a-nasal-orgasm gaze settled on Lindsey. "Hey!"

Before she could reply, he grabbed the bag and headed across the hall and into his office, motioning with his head for her to follow. "Come. Join me."

She groaned but trailed after him.

Underlying music thrummed, meditative and medieval, in the background. Every time Lindsey heard it, she imagined primitive natives dancing around a fire, chanting, and beating their drums…right before they cut the heart out of a sacrificial virgin in the name of some manic rooster god. Stewart claimed he liked to lie on the office couch and "become one" with the music. It gave him time for "introspection and reflecting." But Lindsey had suspected for weeks that Stewart got laid on the couch, and the only thing he "became one" with was Cindie.

Lindsey didn't have solid evidence…yet. But along with the arrival of Stewart's new secretary had come long hours at work, frumpier-than-usual clothes, his weird new diet, an odd affection for drum chants, and lots of meals at the office. The coincidental life changes created a clearer picture than the best Canon on the market. Her day of reckoning awaited.

Stewart rummaged through the bag, placing the items on his desk. Vegetable spring rolls with hemp tofu sauce, kimchi, natto. He frowned and popped the lid of a large plastic bowl, releasing the smell to waft out uninhibited. The stench, almost visible to the naked eye, attacked Lindsey. Her runny nose turned into a torrent of snot, and her pupils shrank to pinpricks as though retreating from Stewart's sustenance.

She glared at her husband's downturned face. "What's the matter?"

He sighed, shook his head, and tapped the ToYuck label stuck to the lid. "I was reading an article about the dirty conditions of this place." He eyed the salad as if the owners of the food processing plant had snuck in and sprinkled botulin toxin on it just to mess with him.

She grabbed the bowl and peered inside. While it smelled like a roadkill smoothie, it still looked like the usual mulch and mixed-weed blend he always ate. She scowled at him. "What are you talking about? What article?"

He plopped into his chair. "Cindie showed it to me. You should read it; you'll never eat pre-packaged food again. The place is disgusting: rats, roaches, and worse. Squalid conditions for the employees. They never clean anything. Failed two of their last three health inspections. Plus, they've been caught using illegal migrant workers."

Her blood started to boil. Stewart's assistant, Cindie, the curly-but-fake-bleached-blonde haired, hundred pound elfin, who wore earthy, billowy dresses and no bra—not that her teacup-sized tits needed any support—health-nut, woman of the soil, everything-has-to-be-organic-and-no-impact-on-mother-Earth hypocritical bitch.

Lindsey referred to the little trollop as *Cindie Brady* or simply *the Elfin*, which, to Lindsey's delight, drove Stewart crazy. Cindie often extolled the healing powers of bean sprouts grown on the side of some mountain in South Africa, which had to be harvested by a virgin medicine woman during the first full lunar eclipse of the year.

The Elfin prattled on about the planet-saving benefits of her homemade, Earth-friendly laundry detergent. "Oh, Lindsey, you should try it. Your clothes smell and feel great. Plus, you have a clear conscience knowing you aren't ruining the habitat for the endangered mole rats of Nicaragua." Or some such nonsense; Lindsey had tuned out right around the time the Elfin had been born.

She'd hated Cindie on sight and loathed her asinine blather about tree-hugging this and eco that. The woman rode a scooter or walked everywhere, ordered everything online from planet-saving sites, paying the premium energy credit to have it shipped via sunbeam, and looked down on anyone who didn't do the same.

Unlike Lindsey, the Elfin had never pushed any linebacker-sized babies through her little Barbie Doll hips, not that she would have even survived such an ordeal. If she'd tried, she probably would have insisted on doing it in a Chinese bath—the water having to have come from a mother effing spring on the top of Mt. Fuji, collected by the damned Buddha himself.

Cindie didn't have to drive kids all over town to various soccer, dance, and football events. Didn't have to do piles of laundry because *no one* in her family knew that it was okay to wear the same set of clothes all day. *Yes, you can put those same jeans you wore to school back on after debate and soccer and football.*

Stewart opened his laptop.

She huffed. "What do you want to eat then?"

He clicked and started typing. "Hmmmm?"

She took several deep breaths to keep herself from shoving his face into the keyboard and slamming the lid on his head. "Lunch." She gave the word special emphasis to highlight his idiocy. "What do you want for lunch?"

He continued typing. "Let's go to Veganismus down the street. Let me finish this email, and we'll leave."

Anxious to be out of the noxious, fume-filled room, Lindsey spun on her heels, but she marched out of the smoke and right into the fire. Cindie sat at her secretary's desk to the left of Stewart's door.

The Elfin gave her a placating smile. "Oh, hi, Lindsey. I thought I heard your voice."

Lindsey considered the merits of ignoring the bitch and walking out of the office, but her pride wouldn't let this wisp of a woman have the satisfaction of seeing her run.

Cindie held out a tissue. "You've got a little something here." She tapped the skin under her little button nose.

Lindsey snatched the tissue and wiped the snot that had collected above her upper lip. *Damn Stewart and his Asian spiced crap.*

"So, Lindsey, I've been meaning to talk to you. As you probably know, Stewie and I are reading this book about holistic child rearing."

"You've what? What book?"

Cindie smirked. "It's one in a series by Dr. Crock. I keep my copy by my bed. Reading it helps me float off to Slumberland, dreaming about the day I get to be as lucky as you and have little ones of my own."

Lindsey pointed then dropped the thumb-hammer of her make-believe gun. "Pa-pow! You can have mine."

The Elfin's shrill little giggle scraped Lindsey's nerves, giving her a rug burn more vicious than the sharpest cheese grater. Cindie's fake smile faded. "Anyway, I wondered if you still let the kids watch TV."

"Huh? Still? What are you talking about?" Lindsey had been prepared for more of the Elfin's organic diet blather, but this question caught her off guard. Her thermostat began to rise again, the mercury pulsing hot and hard through the veins in her forehead as she glared down at the little waif.

"Well…" Cindie had either missed or blatantly ignored the Charles Manson look in Lindsey's eyes—the one that could peel wallpaper and kill small mammals with its laser-like intensity. Even Stewart knew to shut up and slink away when he saw *The Look.* But Cindie either hadn't cared or had simply been too stupid to realize the danger, so she plowed on.

The Elfin folded her hands on her desk and assumed a professorial voice. "According to Dr. Crock, U.S. children watch five hours of TV a day and even more on the weekends. That's one of the reasons all the other countries of the world are passing us intellectually."

She pointed at Lindsey as if driving home a particularly

vital piece of information. "Did you know the average fourth grade child in Asian countries actually scores better than most U.S. high school seniors in both math and science?" She held up her hands. "Why, the Chinese can't even *afford* the TVs they make! Instead, they use that time for meditation and studying the ancient arts of their ancestors. And the children spend at least three hours a day working with their parents."

Cindie reached over and placed her hand on Lindsey's arm. "Usually with their *mom*, on homework, religion, and family values."

The Elfin dropped the hand Lindsey had been about to bite and placed it on her hip. She'd tapped her lips with a chewed, rough fingernail. "You know, they really have that right too. We are so messed up here in the west with all our conflicting religions vying for your dollar. They just have the one religion over there, at least they did before missionaries from the U.S. decided to 'help' them 'see' things our way." She did air quotes for both "help" and "see."

Lindsey "saw" red. Her brother had died serving his country. She seethed over the ungrateful hypocrisy of this hussy putting down the nation that gave her little immigrant ass the freedom to say such things. Nothing short of jumping up on the Elfin's desk, wrapping her hands around the woman's scrawny little neck, and squeezing until her itty bitty eyes popped like champagne corks could have adequately expressed Lindsey's disapproval of the Elfin's foreign policy opinions. *Here are some family values for you, Cindie Effing Brady. How would you like to discuss these ideas with your ancestors personally?*

Stewart walked out before his wife committed a felony and must have summed up the situation—Stalin vs. Gandhi, David vs. Goliath, Hitler vs. Muhammad—because he guided

Lindsey away from a scene that could have resulted in her incarceration.

Lindsey took a deep breath and snatched her arm away from his grasp. "Where are my containers?"

"What containers?"

Why do the stupid seem to be so drawn to me? Do I have "dolt magnet" written on my forehead or something? "The bowls your lunch was in. You know, the meal I brought for you that you aren't going to eat."

Stewart shrugged. "I guess I left them in the office." He paused, looking at her as though he expected praise for remembering to pull his pants up after taking a dump.

Lindsey rolled her eyes. "No. No. Don't trouble yourself. I'll go get them."

"I…"

But she'd already marched away. She stomped past the Elfin—who didn't bother to look up from texting on her phone—and stormed into Stewart's office. As she began to pack the bowls into the bag, she knocked the ToYuck container that had so offended her husband onto the floor. Stewart hadn't fastened the lid and seaweed soufflé spilled onto the carpet.

To keep from screaming in frustration, she rolled her head back and stared at the ceiling while rubbing her neck. *One… Two… Three… Four… Five…* When she reached ten, she grabbed some napkins from the bag and began to sop up the mess. She had to choke down the bile in her throat that threatened to make her lose her gorge right along with the disgusting concoction…not that there would be much difference between her vomit and Stewart's lunch.

She scooped up the first batch of goo then paused when something shiny caught her eye.

Lindsey reached further under Stewart's desk and retrieved a small foil pouch. *Intense Pleasure Organic to Orgasmic.* Her mind raced. New secretary. New couch. Long hours. Now a used condom wrapper. All these added up to a lying, cheating bastard.

Leaving the napkins and mess on the floor, she stood, spied a letter opener on the desk, and started to reach for it. She paused just before her fingers wrapped around the shiny but potentially lethal metal stake that would both free her from this humiliation and also land her behind bars for the rest of her life.

She sucked in a lungful of air as she pulled back her hand. *He's not worth it. You will find another way to get back at him, but going to prison isn't it.* She tucked the damning little foil pouch into her purse and walked out of the office. Her mind floated like a balloon, tethered to the rest of her by the thinnest of ribbons—as though her conscience and her body had become two separate things.

Stewart saw her coming and pressed the button for the elevator. As the doors slid open, he tried to grab her elbow and guide her in. Lindsey yanked her arm free. "I'm not in the mood for lunch. You'd best go by yourself."

Stewart held up his hands. "What's the matter, Linds? Are you still upset by what Cindie said? You really need to get over that." He moved as though to join her, but she shoved him back. "I said, I'm not in the mood to eat."

Lindsey shot daggers out of her eyes until he shook his head and stepped back, and then she pressed the down button.

He offered a limp wave as the door closed. "Hey, I thought you were getting the dishes…"

On the ride to Stewart's office, Lindsey had stuffed the foul concoction her husband called a lunch into the back of the car. But after several such deliveries, the smell had seeped into the upholstery, split open the plastic and rubber trim, and rusted the hull of the vehicle.

The odor haunted the car like a poltergeist. No one wanted to ride with her anymore—not her friends, not her kids, even the cat objected more than usual on the way to the vet. The menacing, unrelenting olfactory phantom assaulted her anew as soon as she climbed into the driver's seat, feeding the flames of her fury with roiling, boiling kerosene.

A scream emanated from deep in her tortured soul, shaking the windows and rattling the dash as her primal fury tore from her throat. She jammed the key into the ignition, slammed the transmission into drive, and peeled out of the parking lot. Squealing around corners and flying down the street, she bypassed the road to their home and drove the eighty miles to Yahatts instead. There, she traded in their conservative Subaru wagon for the largest hulking piece of Detroit chrome and steel the U.S. auto industry had to offer.

She'd walked into the dealership, seen the beast, asked if it came in leather, and said she'd take it. After that, Lindsey had driven the hulking monstrosity from the lot to an electronics superstore, where she'd purchased the largest Chinese-made, flat screen TV they had in stock.

This year's Christmas cards would picture her and the kids dressed in camo, posed in front of their new SUV with a dead deer strapped to the hood, each holding a rifle and a turkey leg.

Merry Friggin' Christmas from the Newmans.

Breaking about every road law created since 1945, Lindsey flew back to town. She didn't slow as she crossed the bridge and directed the beast to Stewart's office. Cindie's little Vespa scooter sat parked on the sidewalk in front of the building. When Lindsey's large vehicle bumped up onto the curb with nary a complaint, she floored the accelerator and aimed down the walkway. With a satisfying crunch, the SUV hit the Vespa, smashing it under large, all-terrain tires.

Lindsey slammed on the brakes, dropped the hulking beast into reverse, and drove over the efficient little mode of transportation again. She smiled as one little scooter wheel rolled pathetically out into the street, pirouetted a couple of times, and then came to rest on its side.

She put the SUV into drive and drove the beast home.

Chapter 2

Lindsey sat cross-legged in the middle of her son's bedroom floor, smoking a joint and reading the love letters he'd received from throngs of infatuated girls. After parking the ginormous gas-guzzler in the driveway—it had taken the space of two regular-sized cars—she'd walked by the hole Mic, her high school senior, called a room. She needed something besides murder to occupy her mind, so she'd started to wade through the debris on the floor, desk, and dresser only to discover a small box hidden in the back of a drawer. Inside she'd found his secret stash of condoms, love letters, and oh-my-god-yes-that-is-pot.

She'd almost closed the lid and tucked it behind the shirts and socks where she'd found it. She'd almost let Mic have his privacy. Almost. Instead, she'd rolled some of the cannabis into a small strip of paper, tucking the ends tight, and lit up.

The grass made her head a little swimmy but took the edge off her fury in a way trading in the car and running over the scooter had not. Her gaze lingered on the glowing end of the stick as she inhaled. It had been at least a year since she'd smoked, but she wouldn't let that much time pass again. *My old friend, oh how I've missed you.* After staring at the red, burning orb for a moment longer, she turned her focus back to Mic's love letters.

Her son, it seemed, had become a lot more popular with the ladies than she'd suspected. The notes gave the impression he hadn't committed to any particular girl and could possibly be having sex with several.

Unlike most mothers, who would have gone ballistic had they discovered their little angels were getting blown behind the bleachers during gym class and mellowing out after school with a bit of Acapulco Red, Lindsey didn't have a problem with it.

He should be experimenting during his high school and college years, though he needed to be careful to not get carried away…like she had.

At her final college party, the one that had changed the course of her life, Lindsey had taken a small handful of the glowing, brightly-colored pills from a bowl of narcotics hodgepodge resembling a Halloween candy mix from Hell.

She'd downed the drugs with vodka, but everything from that point until the next morning—when she woke up in a park, naked save for a thin, dirty blanket wrapped around her slender frame—had been a complete blank. When she'd tried to sit up, she'd found her head glued to the ground by a thick, hard crust. She'd yanked, pulled, and then peeled her face from the lawn. Clumps of dirt and grass had stuck to her cheek, and she'd discovered the source of the adhesive: Dried vomit. Her vomit.

For some reason she could not remember, she'd left the party naked and wandered around until passing out in some random park. She'd not only thrown up on herself but continued the humiliation when she also found a piece of dried up dog crap in her hair. She had been so out of it, so unaware of her surroundings, that she'd lain her head in a bed of shit.

She could have choked to death on her own puke, after

taking only god-knew what and hooking up with only god-knew who, but that piece of feces had tipped her over the edge. She'd set herself straight after that: gotten a job and gone back to school. Not long thereafter, she'd met Stewart—Safe. Predictable. Secure.—and, after a few months of dating, let him talk her into marriage.

She shuddered at those memories from her final year in college. She wanted to yell at the sad, former party girl in this mental horror movie. Tell her to turn back and go a different direction. But she'd continued to march forward toward her own damnation and condemnation, with a stubborn streak the size of Stewart's ego.

Lindsey took a long drag on the joint to calm her nerves and stifle the scream of a wasted life threatening to tear from her lungs. She would talk to Mic, not about the evils of sex and drugs, but about not letting go of the fundamental core that made him Mic. Sometimes lines needed to be crossed and boundaries pushed. He needed to do everything, try everything his heart desired, and never compromise himself… like she had. That one instance had scared her into betraying herself. Now she served a sentence handed down by a judge and jury of one: her. Mic needed to step over his own lines, but he must never, ever, shoehorn himself into a life where he didn't belong.

She wanted better for her son than a domestic imprisonment, married to an uncaring, cheating warden.

Lindsey stuffed the letters into the box and tucked the small container underneath Mic's shirts in the back of the dresser's third drawer. She closed his door, leaving his room in the same despondent disarray in which she'd found it.

The old party girl, whose heart still beat within Lindsey despite being pushed into the back of the third drawer of her mental dresser, screamed for relief and a way out. Revenge.

The fundamental part of her yearned to prove that though irrelevancy had consumed her, it hadn't yet digested and shat her out. The essence of Lindsey—fun, crazy, and free—still raged and clawed like a feral wildcat at the face of apathetic monotony. Twenty years of familial incarceration claimed to have put her into the ground.

She would prove it wrong.

Chapter 3

Lindsey plugged her free ear with her thumb as she confirmed the order with Michelangelo's Pizza for a double-stuffed, all meat, extra-cheese, super-sized pie. Mic had called saying that he would be bringing home a friend from football practice, and she had no intention of cooking.

Stewart had also called and said he'd be late. Good, because it meant she wouldn't have to listen to his blather about Cindie and her organic vaginal yeast protein shakes or whatever they'd been discussing since Lindsey had stormed out. Also good because it meant he wouldn't be pressuring her to make some kind of seaweed and rutabaga casserole for dinner. Bad because she'd been looking forward to the inevitable argument that would ensue because of the new SUV.

She ran through the litany of their pending fight in her mind. Stewart had no inkling of the hell she would descend upon him when she pulled out the condom wrapper. It would be as if the demons in Lucifer's army had all coordinated a break dance party on his soul.

"Hey, mom!" A voice carried from the front of the house, followed by the slamming of the door. "Mom?"

"In the kitchen. Take off your cleats, and don't get dirt on the carpet."

Football gear hit the floor, and then her son barreled into the kitchen with the same subtlety as an enraged bull at a yoga class, shattering all semblances of silence and tranquility in his path. "Mom! Mom! Whose truck is that in the driveway?"

"Ours."

An exuberant smile spread across Mic's face. "What? Really? When did you do that?"

Her son danced from foot to foot, and she smiled at his young-pup excitement over something as trivial as a new car. "This afternoon."

He pumped his fist in the air. "Yes! Thank you! Thank you! Thank you! You have no idea how hard it was to pick up girls in the yellow bomber."

Lindsey shook her head. "I'm sure." Though based on the letters she'd read, the old car hadn't been much of a hindrance to his love life.

He stared at her, eyes wide. "I can't believe dad let you buy it."

She grinned. "He doesn't know yet."

Mic's jaw dropped open, and his arm fell to his side. "What? He's going to connip."

"Probably."

He laughed. "Then his head's going to spin 'round while he spews pea green soup like that possessed chick from that movie."

She chuckled. "And his eyes will melt…"

"…and his hair will stick straight out like he's being electrocuted and then it'll all fall out."

"Then his bones will turn to jelly, and he'll fall on the floor a blob…"

Mic wiped away tears from his eyes as the laughter took hold of him. "And his moobs will start leaking…"

"Again."

They both doubled over, holding their stomachs as their combined amusement filled the small space.

He got control of himself and fist bumped her. "Anyway, even if it means dad turns into a pea-soup-spewing, bald, moob-leaking blob, I'm glad you got us some new wheels."

She shrugged. "Sometimes sacrifices must be made for the greater good. By the way, is your friend coming? Since it's your last day of practice, I ordered a ginormo pizza to celebrate." He'd taken the end of his football career well and found a good first-job at one of the tourist traps in town. Before the hell of today, she'd wanted to be at the final practice in case he required her emotional support. Fortunately, her son didn't need her maternal therapy. He would charge into the unknown—fearless and bold—and never look back…just like his mother used to.

Mic raised his fist into the air again. "Yes! I think I've died and gone to that great guy heaven in the sky where the girls are easy, the cars are fine, and the food is covered in pepperoni and cheese. Yeah, Dios is upstairs getting cleaned up. He asked to use our shower. I hope you don't mind, but I told him it was alright."

She paused and wrinkled her nose. "Yeah. I supposed that's fine. What position does he play on the team? I don't recall anyone by that name being on the roster."

A quizzical expression crossed her son's face. "Huh? Oh, he's not."

"He's not? Not what?"

Mic continued to shed gear, dropping it on the floor and splattering dirt and mud from his uniform across the linoleum. "Neither. He's not my friend, and he's not on the team. He's the assistant football coach."

Lindsey put her hand on her son's shoulder to stop him

from undressing in the middle of the kitchen. "I don't understand. Why are you bringing the coach home?"

"*Assistant* coach. And dad called and asked me to." Mic shrugged as if this explanation made sense.

She shook her head, trying to make the connections between her son's fragmented thoughts. "Please start from the beginning."

Mic sighed. "Dios is the assistant football coach. He started mid-season, which is why you probably never heard of him." He lowered his voice as though eavesdroppers lurked in every corner. "Supposedly he was in community college for four years but kept flunking the general requirements. His mom went back to Peru a few years ago when her visa expired, and he burned through all the money she left him. Someone pulled some strings and got him the assistant's job so he doesn't have to be all pathetic and live with his aunt." He glanced around, still looking for spies and gossip magazine columnists. "Word is, his aunt slept with the vice principal and that's how Dios got the job."

Lindsey furrowed her brow. "Interesting I suppose, but what's that got to do with you, and why, for god's sake, would your dad ask you to bring him here?"

Her son grinned as though he were about to deliver the best fart joke of his life. "His aunt is Cindie from dad's work."

Lindsey reeled back as if her son had bopped her in the nose. "What? Seriously?"

Mic nodded. "Yep. Dad asked me to bring Dios here so he can give them both a ride home tonight. Usually she comes by the school and picks Dios up, but someone demolished her scooter today." He slapped his hands together. "Smashed it flat."

She laughed. "Is that so? Awww that's too bad. Anyway, the pizza gal said their orders are backed up. Probably won't be for another hour. You've got time to go get cleaned up first."

Mic bounded from the room. "Okay, Mom. Hope you ordered two. I'm starving." He galloped up the stairs as lithe as a stampeding rhino.

Lindsey laughed as she imagined the Elfin standing over her beloved, well-flattened scooter. She pulled a beer out of the fridge and popped the top as the shower in the guest bath snapped off.

So odd just coming over and using someone's shower like that. Maybe it's a Peruvian custom? Frigging bitch isn't just invading Stewart's work, now she's got her trailer trash family invading my home.

Well, whatever the custom, she wouldn't let it happen. Enough was enough. She'd march in there and tell Dingo or whatever his name was that he could just leave.

She stomped up the stairs and flung open the door to the guest bath, but it stood empty. Maybe she'd heard Mic's shower?

Just as she turned to march toward Mic's room, a noise in her bedroom drew her attention. She stalked across the vast expanse of carpet ready to give this creepy, lurking boy a piece of her mind. But when she reached the doorway of her bathroom, she froze.

A Greek God of a man, cast by the mighty hammer of Thor himself, stood naked and wet on the shower rug drying his coal-black hair.

Six feet and some change, his olive skin glistened in the rays cast by mirrored vanity lights. Lean and cut with just the right amount of muscle—not big, but well-defined with ridiculous abs. She drank him in as her gaze traveled over the length of his body. Then her eyes widened as visions of horses and Brahma bulls charged through her imagination.

It took her a minute before she realized he'd stopped drying off and now stared back at her, towel mid-fluff. As her eyes rose to meet his—*Eyes up here!* she would have said had a man been ogling her the way she ogled him now—a mischievous grin played across his lips. He wrapped the towel around his waist. "You must be Mrs. Newman."

"And you must be… Ummmm…"

"Emigdio, but every calls me Dios. Nice to meet you, Mrs. Newman." His silky smooth voice and spicy accent drizzled like melted pepper butter across her synapses.

In the distance, she heard herself mutter, "Lindsey, please. Mrs. Newman is Mic's grandmother."

As she guided her misfiring body out of the large bathroom, she bumped into the wall. Dios smiled and placed his hands on his hips. The seam of the towel opened, exposing one well-formed thigh. He made no move to prevent the woman he'd just met from leering at him like a prized slab of beef in a butcher's shop.

Lindsey regained her senses enough to finish navigating her bedroom and close the door. She leaned up against the wall, breathing as though she'd just run a marathon.

Chapter 4

Lindsey lounged on the couch, nursing her second beer of the evening while staring out the front window. As her mind lingered on the beautiful man in her bathroom, her skin flushed hot and rosy. Her nipples grew so perky she could have poked someone's eye out with one.

She needed to focus and gather her wits. So, she took a deep breath, relegated the visions of cut abs and olive-colored skin to the back of her mind, and centered the crosshairs of her thoughts on the impending confrontation. Marking off her mental checklist, she internally battled wits with her accountant husband. He would waltz in, smug as a junkyard dog eager to play with an easy-pickings cat. But he'd discover that his little feline had a shotgun, a lioness set of teeth, and a chew-your-ass attitude. She had both barrels loaded and cocked, the scope sighted and eager for a target. *Pa-pow, Stewie.*

Stewart's pink Fiat pulled half into the driveway and stopped, blocked by the giant SUV taking the space of two regular vehicles. He'd ordered the miniature car with the custom paint job, claiming the color to be "salmon," and each time she'd called it anything else, he'd corrected her. He could call it whatever helped put a pong in his pogo stick, but the car gleamed a brilliant hot pink in the descending sun. The little girl-mobile backed out into the street and slid in next to the curb.

Her husband and the Elfin crawled out of the roller skate. He scowled as he walked around the gas-guzzling behemoth that had taken his parking space, the Elfin trailing in his wake. Halting, he scratched his head and stared at the smudge of purple paint on the bumper—the only evidence linking Lindsey to Cindie's Vespa. The Elfin cocked her head as she too looked at the slight imperfection on the otherwise flawless chrome and steel bumper.

Realization must have penetrated her teeny little brain because Cindie covered her mouth and pointed. She turned her attention to Stewart and began to gesticulate as though signing for a tobacco auctioneer. The window prevented her words from penetrating the house, but based on the flap of her jaw and the angry glare of her eyes, the little nymph gave the lying, cheating prick a scorching earful. Lindsey smiled at their consternation, content in this oasis of amusement as the couple battled it out on her front yard.

Stewart, who looked ready to burst like an over-inflated balloon in the heat of August, said something to Cindie and pointed towards his little car. She stomped her foot, folded her arms, and turned her back. He said something else. She huffed but began clomping her way to the little Fiat.

Lindsey chuckled. *Huh. Not only does she have the tits of a three-year-old, she acts like one too. Way to pick 'em, Stewie.*

Stewart marched toward the house, his jaw set, swinging his arms like an Olympic speed walker. But before he reached the door, another car, this one with a triangular pizza delivery sign on its roof, pulled up. Her husband turned his attention to the approaching kid, who held up a receipt. Stewart's faced turned as red as a fire engine, and he barked something. The angry tone punctured through the big picture window, though the words themselves remained indecipherable. Not shrinking from the onslaught, the kid just shrugged, pointed at the receipt, the house, and then at the pizza. Stewart yanked out his wallet and thrust some money at the delivery boy before grabbing the pie box and continuing to pound toward the front porch.

He glared through the window as he tried to open the door, but Lindsey had left both the handle and thumb-bolt latched. She raised her beer toward him as if making a toast in his honor and took another long pull from the bottle, but she didn't move nor try to help as her husband balanced the huge flat box while working the locks.

The key rattled, and then Stewart flew inside. "You could have at least opened the door when you saw me coming." He slammed it behind him with his foot, dropped the pizza onto the table, and whirled around to her. "Whose ozone-killing monstrosity is that in the driveway? I should have it towed."

"I wouldn't do that." She took another sip from her beer.

He put his hands on his hips. "Oh? And why not? Whose is it?"

Lindsey smiled. "Why, Stewie, it's yours."

Spittle flew from his lips, and his eyes bulged. "Mine?"

She waved her hand back and forth between them. "Well, ours. You know, what's mine is yours and all that." She glanced out the window. The conversation bored her more than she had anticipated it would. She'd already played and replayed this moment so many times in her head that the reality fell flat.

The little muscles in his face spasmed, contorting his features like a cartoon character. "You…you…you…what? Just went to the lot and got that thing without asking me?"

"Yep." Lindsey continued to watch out the front of the house. The Elfin sat in the passenger seat of Stewart's prissmobile, staring at something in her lap—most likely her cell phone. An unhappy frown graced her thin little lips.

Awww poor thing. Best turn that frown upside down, or it'll freeze to your face. Lindsey turned back to her husband, noting his disheveled clothes and flushed complexion, as though he'd run home in his suit and tie instead of driving the three miles and some change.

He waved a slender finger at her as though lecturing a child. "Did you run over Cindie's Vespa?"

She smirked and fluttered her eyelashes. "Oh, was that her little scoot scoot? I thought I felt a bump. I came by your work to show you our new car, but then I changed my mind and thought I'd surprise you tonight instead. I know how much you like surprises, Stewie." She cupped her chin and tapped her teeth. "Hmmm, might have accidently nudged the Elfin's trike when I was in the parking lot."

He waved his hands in the air. "Nudged? Bumped? Are you serious? Her scooter is completely flattened!"

"Can it be fixed? I think one of the wheels or something rolled out into the street. Don't forget to get that when you take it to the repair shop."

Stewart's arms stopped mid-wave, and his jaw dropped open, though no words came out.

Lindsey continued to tap her teeth with her finger. "Oh, I almost forgot. There's a new TV in the back of the car. Can you bring it in and set it up when you have a few minutes?"

Steam didn't actually shoot from the man's ears, but if it had been possible, it would have. "Do I even know you? You smash a perfectly restored vintage Vespa, buy a new car and a TV, and don't even think to ask me first."

She smiled at him and took another pull on her beer. She'd been wrong; the conversation had turned out to be interesting after all. "Well, I didn't even think to ask you if you wanted a turn running over the little harlot's tricycle. Next time I'll check with you."

"Next time?" More spittle flew. Fortunately he stood several feet from her, or she'd be taking a spit shower. "There won't be a next time. I don't know what's gotten into you, Lindsey, but here's what's going to happen." He ticked off the points on his fingers. "First, you're going to go out there and apologize to Cindie. She loved that scooter, and now she's completely distraught. The cost of replacing it, by the way, will come out of *your* household expenses. Then, in the morning, you're taking the TV and that…that…thing in the driveway back to wherever the hell you bought it and getting our Subaru and our money back."

She looked her husband in the eyes. "No."

He reeled back. "No?"

Lindsey shook her head. "No."

Stewart looked as though she'd spoken in Latin. "What do you mean?"

She got up, set down her beer, and walked over to her purse. She fished around inside, retrieving the small aluminum foil pouch she'd found under his desk. She turned and faced him, took his hand, and placed the empty condom envelope in his palm. "I have a get out of jail free card, Stewart. You aren't calling the shots anymore. I am."

As he stared at the little piece of foil, the angry red color drained from his face leaving him pasty white. "Linds, I can explain…"

She held up her hand. "No. No, you don't need to. I get it."

"It's not mine…"

Lindsey cocked her head and narrowed her eyes.

"Okay, okay." He took her hand in both of his soft, accountant ones. "Yes, it's mine. It's…it's…just that things haven't been right between us for a while. And I've been working long hours…and we…um…well one night one thing led to another…and…"

She shook her head and placed her finger over his lips. "Please stop talking. You're an embarrassment to lying, cheating bastards everywhere." Earlier, Lindsey had expected

to tear Stewart a new asshole the second he walked through
the door. But as day turned to dusk an odd, perplexing
calm had overcome her. But the cool demeanor shrouded a
simmering anger, a buildup of pressure, like two faults on the
brink of erupting into a California-sliding-into-the-ocean
earthquake.

This placidness should have scared her husband more than
her fury. But instead of scampering away, he had tried to lie
his way out of the situation. This didn't surprise her, though it
did add more fuel to her quiet rage.

He dropped to his knees, eyes pleading. "We can work this
out. I don't think there's any reason to go rushing to a lawyer
and doing something rash." Then almost as an afterthought,
he added, "I…I…I still love you."

She didn't know what she hated more, him lying about
feelings he clearly no longer possessed, that he'd already
thought about what she and her lawyer might take from
him, or that he'd resorted to a sniveling, pathetic little beggar.
The loser before her didn't look at all like the safe, practical,
considerate man she'd married. She searched for sympathy, a
shred of affection for this sorry sack of garbage, but came up
empty. "You're right, Stewart. No need to do anything rash."

A hopeful wisp of a smile played across his lips.

She took a long breath and, unable to bear looking at him
on the floor, pulled him to his feet. "Here's what you're going
to do." She pointed out the front window. "First get that
piece of trash off of our curb. Take her back to whatever rock
she crawled out from under. When you get home, you're
going to pack your things and move your ass into the den.
Don't talk to me, don't look at me, don't even breathe around
me, or you'll find yourself living under the same rock as your
whore. Is that clear?"

He bobbed his head as though his neck had turned into a
muscleless spring.

She pointed at the hallway then jerked her thumb at the door. "Her nephew is upstairs. Get him and get the hell out of here. Hopefully your key will still work when you get back."

As her husband spun and bounded up the stairs, Lindsey returned to her place on the couch and paid no attention when Stewart and Dios trudged through the living room and out the front door. She shook her head at the idiocy of the two men trying to maneuver the large Peruvian into Stewart's joke of a car. After several failed attempts, her husband opened the hatchback. Dios looked unsure but crawled in and fell into the back seat.

Stewart slammed the trunk then stopped. His eyes found hers. For a moment, their gaze locked. A fleeting ping of the love she'd once felt for this man chimed in her heart. As the long, melodious tone finished its final vibration and became silent once more, it signaled the end of her affection and the closing of a chapter in her life. Her husband blinked, breaking their connection, got into his car, and drove away.

As he putted down the avenue, the tail lights of the Fiat twinkled in the dwindling twilight then winked out, vanishing as if they'd never been there. The physical distance between husband and wife mimicked the emotional chasm that had taken root and grown over the years—fertilized by apathy, disappointment, and regret. Lindsey swiped at her cheek, surprised when her fingers came away wet from tears that no one—least of all her—would have believed she had in her.

As soon as Stewart got his crap out of their room, she would take a sleeping pill and slip into a coma for about a week. She got up from the couch, tossed her empty bottle into the trash, and headed up the stairs.

Lindsey and sleep remained strangers despite the powerful sedative. For a long time, her mind lingered on the fight with Stewart. It hadn't just been the pathetic way he'd rolled over or the things he'd said, but the things that he hadn't said that bothered her most. For instance, if he really still loved her, shouldn't he have at least offered to fire the little harlot he spent almost every day with? With so much at stake, why keep her around? Also, he should have asked to go to counseling and work on "us." That's what people did who still loved each other.

But Lindsey would have rather pounded her head into the wall until her skull cracked like a clay pot against a cinderblock than sit in a therapist's office listening to Stewart blather about how his wife didn't support him and how Cindie loved and accepted him. Lindsey didn't want to try and go back to when they'd felt something besides distance and animosity. She'd given up her live-free, party-hard identity and adopted a June Cleaver set of morals and ethics that fit the regimented life of kids, work, and domestic divaship. But the thing that had allowed her to survive in such a warped and mundane existence had snapped when she found the empty condom wrapper under her husband's desk. And even if she could fix whatever had been broken, she wouldn't try.

She needed to find herself. Find a new purpose. Find a new throne on which to perch her ass.

As she rolled onto her back, she dismissed thoughts of Stewart, the Elfin, and the whole disaster, and instead returned to the bathroom and the beautiful man…and his extraordinary endowments. Lean muscles flexing beneath dark skin. Hard abs and jet-black hair. But what revved Lindsey's engine like a Formula One car had been the way his dark eyes had fixed onto hers as he flashed her that unembarrassed, sly little grin. If only he could keep her company on the lonely afternoons…

Her eyes popped open, and her breath caught in her throat. A prospect, an idea…and the incredible possibilities that stretched both legal and moral boundaries flashed into her mind as if she'd flipped over a playing card. But instead of aces and clubs, it had her as the queen of hearts, under the title *A New Life*.

Flipping the idea around, she examined it from all angles. The details still needed to be hammered out, but the concept worked. The universe coalesced, as if everything she'd done, everything she'd suffered, had led to this moment. As fundamental as the breaking of her old life had been in Stewart's office, this idea fulfilled her destiny.

This ploy, if she didn't handle it just right, could land her in jail, but she could deal with the sheriff. She smiled as she imagined Pastor Rose's butthole puckering and the conservatives of the town choking on their own self-righteous bile if they ever learned of her thoughts. It was badass. It was fun. It was risky. In other words, it was all Lindsey.

She'd planned on going to Hell anyway, so she may as well put the top down, step on the gas, and enjoy the ride to eternal damnation in style. She may burn forever, but at least she'd have interesting yarns to spin as she and the other sinners mined brimstone together.

Chapter 5

With her son gone to his new job and her daughter at debate, Lindsey waited for Stewart to call to say he would be working late so she'd have the house to herself for the evening. As she made preparations, she kept an eye on the clock. At exactly three thirty, her phone played the first few dramatic bars of "Taps," her husband's ringtone.

"Hey, Linds." Primitive jungle music thrummed just beneath his words as though after their call he planned to strap on a leather loin cloth and prance around a bonfire.

She took a deep breath. "Hey. What's up?"

"Just letting you know, Jim's books are way behind, so I'm probably going to be staying later than usual. He's got…"

"Do what you need to do, Stewart." She didn't need to hear his detailed ramblings to grasp the plot of the tale he spun. Besides, accounting-world stories made her want to shove an icepick through her temple.

"Thanks. I was worried you'd be upset with what's been going on with us and stuff. But there's just so much to do. He hasn't entered any receipts since…"

She rolled her eyes. "Okay, go enter your receipts. See ya later. 'Night." And she snapped the phone shut, cutting off his blather before it melted her brain.

Stay away as long as you want, Stewie. In fact, why don't you and Cindie put on an extra CD and bonk to the rhythm of the conga all night.

With the house secure, the old party girl raged inside the domestic goddess, lusting to take control. Lindsey let it. Asleep for decades, the untamed animal roared with a victory cry so fierce it could have been leading a thousand men on horseback into battle.

She smiled sphynx-like as she flipped the phone back open and began to punch in numbers.

Lindsey's eyes drank in every detail as the man's muscles flexed and rippled through his tight t-shirt.

She pointed. "Put that one up there."

"Yes, Mrs. Newman." He carried the heavy box to the space she'd indicated and deposited it on the shelf.

She twirled her finger. "Oh, can you turn it around so the label's in the front? Otherwise I'll have to take it down again to see what's in it."

His biceps bulged as he pulled the large box out and flipped it around. "Sure thing, Mrs. Newman."

Lindsey smiled at him, nodding in approval. *The boy is obedient. This just might work. Anyone else would have asked her to open the garage door to let in a breeze, but he didn't.* She needed just the two of them together without the world outside watching. "Can you put that one up there? You're tall, but you'll still need something to stand on."

He grabbed a nearby ladder and popped it open. His jeans strained to contain the muscles of his quads as he ascended the steps and hoisted the last of the boxes onto the storage rack. Turning around, he sat on the top wrung, propping one leg up while letting the other dangle. He smiled down at her.

If the aliens came seeking a perfect physical specimen, they would be entranced by this beautiful embodiment of all things mansome and virile.

"Anything else, Mrs. Newman?"

Yes. Can you get an extinguisher? I think my underwear is on fire. She swallowed to wet her parched throat. "First, please, for the sake of my sanity, call me Lindsey."

She took a deep breath. "And second, yes, yes there is." She reached up, took his large hand, and pulled. He hopped down from the ladder but kept possession of both her hand and her gaze.

The party animal's heart beat like a war drum. *Cancel that fire extinguisher. You just made me dowse the blaze in my own panties.*

She took his face in her hands and kissed him. At first, he hesitated, but then he smashed their lips together and thrust his tongue into her mouth.

She shoved him away, wiping her face with the back of her hand. "Ugh. What was that? You are not a Neanderthal, and I'm not a prize buck you're dragging back to your cave. Go gently, at least for right now, like this." She touched her lips to his, skimming their surfaces together.

As their kiss lingered, his hands found her waist, and though strong, he kept his embrace firm but not too tight. He followed her instructions and didn't maul her with his lips this time. Just below the surface, a raw sexual tension emanated through his fingers, in the heat of his breath, and the aroma of his body, steaming through her in a delicious torrent of carnality.

He's a beast…but he can be tamed and trained. She broke the kiss. Longing and desire blazed in his eyes.

She wrapped her arms around his neck. "We can do this, but there are a couple of rules. The first one is you tell no one. Ever. Not Mic, not your friends, not your aunt, not your rabbi."

He nodded.

"Second, you do *exactly* as I say. You do it without question and only when I tell you. Don't come over unannounced; don't do anything unless instructed to do so. If you can't live with these rules, you need to go home right now, and we'll forget this ever happened."

When he tilted his head and paused, a jolt of anticipation ran through her. But then that sly smile, the one that raised goosebumps on her nether quarters, spread across his pouty lips, and her inner party animal raised a tequila shot into the air, slammed it, and did a touchdown victory dance. He took her hand and kissed the back of it.

Dios' black eyes never left hers. "What would you like me to do first?"

Lindsey took his hand and led him from the garage into the house. After closing the door, she stopped in the living room while he continued on toward the stairs.

She raised an eyebrow and crossed her arms. "Just where do you think you're going?"

He ducked his head like a kid who'd gotten caught eating a cookie for breakfast and motioned toward the stairway. "I… um…well…we…um…"

She suppressed a laugh. In her hands, she possessed the ultimate lump of clay, and like a master potter, she would mold and shape him, creating a work of art that would rival anything Michelangelo ever chiseled out of granite. He had the perfect, God-given physical attributes and a willingness to learn, but she had much to teach him.

She put her hands on her hips. "What? You think I'm going to let you kiss me then I'll just follow you up to the bedroom?"

"You kissed me…" He dropped his gaze back to the floor as he trudged back over to her.

She lifted one side of her mouth in a half-smirk. "Yes, I suppose I did. But we have a long way to go before we ever hit the sheets." She lifted his chin and pointed to his eyes. "Seduction begins with the eyes. Engage. Always look at me directly. Like you did when you kissed my hand. That was perfect."

"Mrs. Newman…er Lindsey, for you, it's easy."

She stared at him. "First of all, don't stutter. It makes my ears bleed. And second, yes, of course it's easy for me. I know what I want, and I'm not afraid to go after it. You should too. Most people don't know what they desire until you show them. Lead them, Dios. You have to make a girl realize the thing she needs more than anything else in the world is you. Understand?"

He frowned. "I think so."

She touched his chin. "No. You don't 'think' anything. Know it. Own it. Okay? Now seduce me."

Gazing into her eyes, he took her hand, kissed it, and yanked her towards him.

Fury and frustration roiled and rolled within her, exploding like a nitro and glycerin cocktail. She stomped on his toe with one sneaker-clad foot. "No!"

"Ouch!" He let her go, grabbing his injured toes.

She marched away and began to pace. "Gawd. You have so much potential, but there is a serious amount of work ahead of us if you keep insisting on trying to Neanderthal me."

He winced, hunching his shoulders at the onslaught. "Sorry."

She crossed back over to him, sighed, and pulled his chin up again. "What did I tell you about looking people in the eyes? You need to be gentle. I don't want to be yanked, dragged, pulled, thrown, or pushed. Lead me. Do you think you can do that?"

He nodded and let out a pent-up breath.

She released his chin and walked around him, swinging her hips and dragging a long finger along his thick chest, over his well-defined bicep, and around to his back. "A girl wants a strong, disciplined man to guide her." She leaned in close, whispering in his ear. "Tell me, Dios, what is the sexiest part of a woman's body?"

He panted while his eyes followed her as though he suffered from severe dehydration and she carried the last drops of life-saving water on Earth. He gulped. "Well, her…um…you know."

She continued to sashay while tracing her finger up his neck, gracing his ear, and along his jaw. "Uh uhhhh. That's part of the problem; you really have no clue." She leaned in and tapped her forehead. "Right here. The journey to the bedroom starts right here between my ears, not between my legs. This is the hottest part of a woman." Lindsey flipped around, leaning her back against his chest, and gave him a sly smile over her shoulder. "No matter how dark and smoldering a look you give her, you can't just gaze into a girl's eyes and romp her. It doesn't work like that."

Lindsey shimmied against him. "Now, tell me this. You're a young buck raging with hormones. Do you watch porn?"

"I…um…I…" His eyes bulged, and he started shaking his head.

She waggled her finger at him. "Uh, uh. What did I tell you about stuttering? Besides, this will only work if you tell me the truth."

He bobbed his head as the denial turned into a nod.

"Of course you do. It's no wonder you thought you could just drag me to your cave. Things in reality don't work like they do in porn-land. Girls don't just wander into a room ready to go. But I will let you in on a little secret, Dios." She turned around, leaned in, and whispered against his neck. "I do want you to claim me. I want you to seduce me." She nibbled on his ear. When he tried to jerk back, she wrapped her arms around his neck and refused to let go.

Lindsey released his ear, giving it a little kiss. Under her touch, a shudder ran through her boy toy's body. She slid her hands to the sides of his face, staring into his dark eyes. "Claim and seduce me, but slowly."

If his eyes get any wider, they'll pop out of their sockets and roll across the floor.

Suppressing a grin, Lindsey stepped away from him and placed her hands behind her back. "Okay, homework time."

He almost fell forward at her sudden movement.

"With the season over, there isn't much need for an assistant football coach right now. So I'm guessing you have a lot of free time on your hands, right?"

He scowled. "They're working on finding more for me to do."

Lindsey raised her eyebrows.

Dios took a deep breath, relaxed his face, and nodded. "They also said it could take a while."

She smiled. "Good. I'm glad you're not busy because I've got a laundry list for you. Here's your first task: I'm going to text you a list of chick flicks. I want you to watch every one of them. The story lines are weak, but observe the way the male characters woo a woman, the way they flirt and look at her. Some of the guys are cute and bumbling; they're pretty ridiculous except they know how to flirt. Pick up some of those techniques, but that is all. I want you to mainly focus on the strong, quiet leaders. Pay close attention to their demeanor and how they take charge of a room when they enter it. These guys have invested millions of dollars in training and have it down to a science. There's a reason every girl on the planet sloshes in her undies watching them. Observe and learn, alright?"

Dios grimaced but agreed.

She nuzzled up to him until their noses almost touched. "Don't worry about your reputation with the guys." She grinned. "I promise I won't tell a soul." After running her hands over his chest, she traced his face with her fingertips one last time. "I'll make it worth your while."

She lingered until he moved to kiss her then she stepped out of his arms and out of his reach. "Go do your homework. I'll send you the list. Text me when you think you've got it."

He took a deep breath, nodded, and left.

Lindsey watched her protégé walk out the front door. Step one of her new life had begun, and she'd done more brilliantly than even she'd expected. The time had come to have a little chat with Sheriff Austin. Her new venture needed protection and a very hands-off mentality from the local law enforcement.

She unzipped her purse, slid her hand deep into a side compartment, and pulled out the small bag of weed she'd procured from a local supplier.

Lindsey smiled, nothing like a little of the sheriff's favorite blend to take the rough edges off a business deal and help with negotiations. The two of them hadn't lit up any Hocus Pocus together since ditching geometry in high school. They could hash out old times while striking a bargain that worked for each of them. She slipped the baggie back into her purse, grabbed the keys to the new SUV, and headed toward the door.

Chapter 6

S low down!" Lindsey shoved Dios' hands off her body. "Why are you grabbing me like you're trying to steal my wallet? Your pleasure comes from the pleasure you give your woman. Take care of her, and she will reward you in ways you can't even imagine. But you *have* to think of her first. *Every time*. Keep control of yourself."

He'd taken two full days to watch all the movies she'd sent him. And though they'd discussed them at great length, some of the more important lessons hadn't stuck.

He cast his eyes down and brought them back up to meet hers again, giving her an impish, embarrassed smile.

She scowled. "Well, at least you remembered to look at me this time." She took a deep breath. "If you grab and manhandle me like you're auditioning for World Wrestling, then I won't even let you get into the ring. And that means you'll have no chance at all of winning the prize. Knock it off. Now, try again."

Dios took her hand with a grip so loose he almost dropped it.

When he brought her fingers up to his lips to kiss them, she snatched her hand back. "Are you gay?"

He stiffened. "Of course not."

"Then knock off the limp wrist crap. It makes me as dry as the Sahara. Don't maul me, but still be a man. Be assertive."

He pulled back his shoulders and straightened his posture. Giving her his sly smile, he lifted her hand and pressed his lips to it.

That's a boy.

He kissed his way up to the crook of her elbow and up to her shoulder. As he moved aside the strap of her tank top, he didn't miss an inch of skin. While Dios traced his tongue from her collarbone to her neck, he ran his fingers through her hair. Lindsey gasped, and her eyes rolled back in her head. Just when she'd started to have hope for her student— that maybe, just maybe, he could be taught after all—he bit her earlobe. Hard.

Lindsey smacked his head and shoved him away. "Gawd, what do you think I am, beef jerky? Don't gnaw on me." She reached over and grabbed his ear, twisting and yanking it towards the floor.

Dios tried to wrestle away from her, but she held tight. "Ouch! Ouch! What are you doing?"

She seethed. "Does this feel sexy to you?" She gave him another extra hard tug.

"No. No, it doesn't." His hands covered his flaming red lobe, and his face turned crimson to match.

"I'm glad you don't think so because neither do I." She shoved his hand away, gave his ear a final tweak, and released him.

He pressed his hand against the side of his head; tears dotted his eyes, but he held himself together.

She glared at her pupil. "Gentle! Now try once more, but if you bite me there or anywhere else again, I'm going to knee you in the nuts so hard your grandsons will sing soprano."

Dios kissed Lindsey's ankle. He ran his thumbs up and

down her calf as he followed behind with his lips. She shuddered when his hot breath brushed her knee. As he continued up the inside of her thigh, her heart hammered. She reached down and ran her hands through his hair.

As his fingers and mouth grazed over the delicate skin between her legs, she arched her back and moaned. He moved higher, kissing the sensitive flesh between her thighs. She moaned even louder. Dios traced the length of her genitals with his tongue, and Lindsey floated in a sea of pleasure. When he pressed harder, her clitoris rolled like an ankle on a loose rock, yanking her out of the moment and thrusting her back into reality.

After another sharp bee sting stab, she cried out. "Ouch! What the hell are you doing?"

He popped his head up. "What? Is this not right?"

She flipped onto her side and sat up. "Oh my gawd. What do you think 'Ouch!' means? How many times do we have to go over this? Gentle! I explain what you are supposed to do and you say you get it, but if you do, you aren't applying it. You can lead me to the place of magic, but you can't force me there. You aren't pushing a car. This isn't about pressure and effort; it's about technique."

Lindsey sighed. She again explained to him what to do and laid back. "Hopefully you didn't rough things up too much. If you did, we'll have to wait for a while. Let's try again."

Soon she'd floated off to her happy place once more…and this time, she stayed there.

The next morning, they sat at her little dining room table drinking coffee. She had several bite marks in various places on her body and, in return, she'd given him more than a few bruises. But over the last couple of weeks, Lindsey's student had made remarkable progress.

She mentally patted herself on the back for taking a handsy, blundering caveman and turning him into a sexual virtuoso. After pouring several packets of artificial sweetener into her brew, she began to stir. The spoon clinked on the side of her cup with each rotation. "Having seduction skills is one thing, but there's a lot more to wooing a woman than just spending time with her in the bedroom. You've got a great smile and a natural poise, but you're going to have to work on your conversation skills."

He arched a perfect eyebrow. "Why?"

She gave him a half-grin over her steaming mug of java. "All in good time. There's a reason for everything I'm teaching you."

He sighed. "Okay, how do we do that?"

She set her cup down and stared at him. "First of all, don't ever, ever sigh and act like you don't care about what I'm saying. You don't need to say much, but you have to act interested. Look me in the eyes, ask questions, and then listen. That's all there is to it."

Dios nodded and took a sip of his coffee, his eyes never leaving hers.

Better. Okay, he's come this far. Bedroom skills, check. Conversation and eye contact, check. That leaves just one thing.

Lindsey continued to stir her coffee and watched as the blend turned from bitter to sweet—much like her pupil. "There's something else. You have to be discreet. It's all about strength and keeping your shit together. If I feel like you're in charge of yourself and in control of the details—a.k.a. you can keep your mouth shut and act normal—then I'm going to feel freer to express myself in the bedroom. But if I'm worried you're going to lose it, you're out the door."

Dios cocked his head like an inquisitive Labrador that didn't quite understand what he saw.

How can I teach this guy this lesson? And then she had it. The party animal within her found the idea crazy and risky but loved it even more for those very reasons. "You know, you're doing well, and we've talked and talked and talked. But the only way to really know if you've got what it takes is to jump into the fire."

Dios tilted his head the other direction.

Pleased with herself, Lindsey grinned and nodded. "Come over for dinner tonight. Eat with the family. Let's put your skills to the test."

He jerked back like she'd slapped him and shook his head. "No, that's not a good idea."

She leaned over the table. "Actually, it's a perfect idea. Be here at seven. Oh, and Dios?"

He raised that same perfect, exquisite eyebrow again.

"I won't be wearing any underwear under my dress."

He sucked in a breath as a slow grin spread across his face.

That evening, the Newmans and their guest sat around the dining room table, laughing and chatting. As Dios discussed the finer points of the Seattle Seahawks' defense strategy with Mic and Stewart, he placed his hand under the tablecloth on Lindsey's bare knee.

She'd been fighting the urge to lay her head in her plate and snore her way through the mundane sports talk, but Dios' movement jolted her awake. Her spoonful of mashed potatoes and gravy halted halfway in between the plate and her mouth. Though she'd instructed him to keep his shit together, she'd underestimated how hard it would be to hang on to her own. Not to be outdone by the Casanova-Frankenstein hybrid of her own creation, she shoved the spoon into her mouth and put on her best poker face.

He traced little circles along the inside of her leg with his fingertips, moving higher and higher up her bare thigh and up under her skirt. She had, as promised, not worn any underwear, and he graced the tufts of exposed hair, teasing her. Then his finger stroked the length of her, lightly tracing the periphery. Lindsey bit her tongue to stifle the gasp threatening to rip from her throat. She set her spoon back on her plate to keep the quivering utensil from announcing to the world that Dios had become Magellan and her body the new frontier.

The ice in her cup rattled as she took a shaky gulp of water. Her daughter glanced up from her phone, though her fingers continued to dance a texting tango across its glowing flat surface. The girl frowned, and her scrutiny flicked from Lindsey to Dios then back to Lindsey. She continued studying her mom's face for a moment, and then the girl's eyes grew wide. A slow smirk spread across her lips. *You've got a secret, and I know what it is*, her eyes said. The mother-daughter gaze locked for an instant longer before the phone buzzed. The teen shrugged and returned to her electronic melodrama.

Lindsey didn't know what to make of the odd encounter and didn't have the wherewithal nor time to think on it further. Dios moved his fingers around in a little circle, slow at first but increasing in speed and pressure…gently as she'd instructed.

In some other universe, her son laughed and her daughter continued to text, but Lindsey drifted away from them to a different plane and dimension. Nothing existed except the butterfly kisses of this skillful man's caress.

As the tension coiled inside her belly and her body began to quake, she flew out of her seat. Startled by the sudden movement, Stewart shot hemp milk out of his nose, and it flew across the table. Fat white drops coated Mic's plate and rolled down the side of his glass. A stream of cream-colored snot dribbled from Stewart's nostrils to the front of his shirt and splattered on his tie.

Her daughter glanced up from her phone, that bitchy little smile still on her lips.

"Gross, Dad!" Mic stared at his ruined dinner while wiping off his arm.

Stewart blotted his face with a napkin. "What the hell, Lindsey? What's the matter?"

She took a deep breath and smoothed her skirt but made no effort to hide the exasperation from her voice. "Nothing, Stewart." She smiled at everyone else. "Excuse me, but I have to go to the bathroom."

Her husband pinched the bridge of his nose as if her very existence irritated him. "Then go already. Why do you always have to make such a big production out of everything?"

After shooting him *The Look*, Lindsey forced herself to not sprint from the room. Walking on rubbery legs, she made her exit down the hall and into the small downstairs bath.

Stewart's voice floated through the door. "Don't use the goat-cheese soap Cindie gave us, the ones shaped like little fruit. I use those on my face at night because they help clear up my acne and moisturize the skin. They are *not* for washing your hands."

Lindsey leaned against the counter and, shaking, wrapped her arms around herself. She didn't care two figs about Stewart's lady soap; the fire Dios had stoked at the dinner table raged and burned within her. She waited. Stewart would leave, as always, without offering to help clean up. The kids would follow.

"Well," her husband said from the dining room. "I have a lot of work to do. It's been a pleasure talking to you, Dino."

"Dios, and the pleasure is mine."

"I've lost my appetite," Mic said.

"Same here," her daughter announced.

Chairs scraped against the floor. Lindsey pressed her ear to the door—clomping, that would be Mic; a lighter footfall, that would be her daughter; and shuffling, that would be Stewart. One by one, they all headed up the stairs. Usually, Lindsey groused all evening after her family left without offering to help cleanup, but tonight, their hasty departure elated her. As soon as the last bedroom door shut, she stormed into the dining room, grabbed Dios' hand, and reversed course back into the bathroom.

Dios closed the door behind him, locking the little brass handle. He took her into his arms, his hands cupping her behind, and lifted her as though she weighed no more than pumice. She wrapped her legs around his waist as she French-kissed her Peruvian boy toy. The roughness of his jeans pressed against her bare thighs almost caused her arousal thermostat to melt down like an out of control nuclear reactor.

His free hand raked through her hair, tousling her blonde curls. As he dipped her back, he kissed her throat and left a blazing path all the way to the bottom of the V-cut in her dress. She wiggled her hips against his, the primal urges driving all thoughts from her mind. His lips turned up into that sly grin as he lifted her onto the counter.

The frigid black granite grabbed her ass like the paw of a snow beast, but her scalding skin heated up the surface and melted the fiend until nothing existed but a puddle. Dios dropped his pants, lifted her skirt, and entered her while the rest of the family went about their business elsewhere in the house. She bit down on a towel to stifle her cry as the orgasm tore through her body.

In the afterglow of their union, she washed with the goat-cheese soap. She admired her hands as she patted them dry. *Stewart's right; this shit really does moisten the skin.*

Chapter 7

The next day, Lindsey and Dios spent the first couple of hours together exploring one another's bodies. After her third orgasm, she settled under the covers and pulled the sheet up to her chin to hide her mischievous grin. She'd done it. She'd taken an unruly, handsy clod and turned him into a suave, romantic seduction-artist.

As they lay naked, post-coitus, and sweat-soaked, her muscles aching, the mirror above her king-sized bed wept with the condensation of their gymnastics. She pushed down the sheet and slinked next to him. Using his flat, hard stomach as a pillow, she traced one defined ab with a long, slender finger. "I was thinking, you need a job, and I need work done around here. Odd jobs, painting, gutters cleaned, gardening, so on."

Dios' voice dripped with drowsiness while he outlined her vertebrae with his thumb. "I don't know much about any of that. I've never been particularly good with my hands."

She sat up, raised an eyebrow, and laughed. "Oh, really? Seems to me you just showed me how fine you are with your hands."

He opened his eyes. Smirking, he touched her cheek for a heartbeat then dropped his hand, cupping her breast.

Though his touch sent electric sparks coursing through her,

she pushed his hand away. They had business to conduct. "It's time for you to start a career."

"I have a job."

She put a hand on her hip, while using the other to keep herself propped up. "Oh, really? I thought we talked about how your *assistant* football coach job is done now that the season's over?"

He shrugged. "Yeah, I guess so. But the vice principal is working on getting me more work. He said I did a good job and have a bright future ahead of me."

"He did, did he?" *Did he even know why he'd been given the position in the first place? Maybe he had no clue that his aunt slept him into a job. Could he really be that dumb? Well, there's a reason he flunked out of school.* She sighed. "Yes, Dios. I supposed that's always an option, but what if something more…lucrative became available."

"So you want me to work for you? Cleaning gutters and stuff doesn't sound very fun to me. It's easier to just help out around the school."

"Seriously? You have to know there's no future in it. If you join forces with me, you'll have a bright, fun future because the work you will actually be doing won't be digging ditches and pouring cement."

He tilted his head, apprehension in his eyes. "It won't? What are you talking about then?"

She smirked. "Let's just say I've been grooming you for this position for a while now."

She began to fill him in on her plan. As if its pigments had begun to flee in terror, his once-olive skin turned the same pallid hue as the sheet around his waist. He tried to interrupt her, but each time, she shushed him, placing a finger over his lips. "Just wait until I'm done. I know what I'm doing."

When she finished her explanation, he remained quiet.

After his relentless attempts to bombard her while she spoke, she'd expected him to verbally vomit his thoughts.

She huffed, vexed by his silence. "Well, before you couldn't seem to shut up. What do you think?"

He raised his brows. "Are you sure it'll work?"

Nodding, she ran a fingernail along his chest and smiled. "I know it will. But we need to get things set up first." She reached for her phone.

He put his hand over hers before she could pick up her cell. "Who are you calling?"

"Stewart." Her smile widened. "This is totally his thing."

Dios shot up like he'd sat on a pinecone. He shook his head as his jaw hung open. "What? What's his thing?"

Lindsey pushed him back onto the bed to keep him from bolting. "Silly boy. I'm calling him to have him do the boring part of setting up the business."

"Umm, now? From here? Like this?" He gestured at their nakedness.

Lindsey chuckled. "You want to put on a coat and tie first? Of course from here and like this." Her gaze traversed the body of the man in her bed as though she planned to make a map and provide guided tours. "Besides, you are my eye candy and will keep me entertained while I talk to the douche." Smirking, she gave him a peck on the lips then dialed.

The phone rang, and then a familiar voice answered. "Hey. What's up?"

"Hey. I've been talking to my friends, and there's a need here in town for a good handyman service." She waggled her eyebrows at Dios. He took a deep breath but remained silent.

"Okay, so what?" Someone said something to her husband, who must have covered up the receiver as he answered, making Lindsey wait for him to complete the muffled conversation.

Irritation flooded her veins, but she took a deep, calming

breath and mentally counted to ten. Instead of allowing her rage to take over the conversation and deluge the little prick in a fire and acid rain shower, she settled her mind and remained focused on her new enterprise. "I'm going to start a business, and I want you to set it up for me. Oh, and you know Cindie's nephew, Dios?" It had taken all of her self-control to refrain from calling Stewart's little girlfriend "the Elfin." Beside her, the Peruvian squirmed.

"Of course I do. We just had him over for dinner the other night." Exasperation tinged his words. At least she had Stewart's undivided attention. She'd said the one thing that would make him drop everything else and focus: Cindie Effing-Dumb-Bitch Brady. This annoyed her even more than when he'd put her on hold.

Through clenched teeth, she forced a pleasant, saccharine tone, trying not to get a cavity from her own fake sweetness. "Anyway, I needed some stuff done around here, so I asked him to help me."

"So he took care of you?"

"Did he take care of me?" She winked at her lover. "Oh yeah, he did a great job. Completely satisfied."

Dios shook his head and made a slashing motion against his throat.

The party girl within Lindsey pushed on. She would get what she wanted and do whatever—and whomever—she wanted. "Anyway, we got to talking, and I'd like to make him my first employee. I need you to file the right papers, get the permits, set up the insurance, and whatnot. Also, I'll need someone to handle the books and do the taxes."

Her husband must have gotten bored because the staccato click of typing resumed. "Uh, sure. I can do that."

"We are going to be a big success. I can attest that he's really skilled at what he does." She wiggled her eyebrows at Dios who dropped his face into his palms. Party Girl

Lindsey raised a glass of vodka to Domesticated Lindsey. The incarcerated housewife had managed to seduce a much younger man and pull the wool over her pansy husband's eyes. Stewie could have his Congo music, goat-cheese soap, and titless mistress while the party girl sweated and moaned in their bed under the talented hands of her Peruvian protégé.

The rustling of papers on the other end of the line stopped. "Are you really sure he's good with that sort of thing? I've never seen him do anything. Besides, I'm not sure the town is ready for someone like him."

She frowned. "Someone like him?"

"A gay handyman."

Lindsey covered the receiver as she burst out laughing. Dios' head snapped up, and he stared at her, his nose wrinkled in confusion. She reeled in her amusement for the sake of the business deal and got herself back under control. "You think so?"

"Really. You know I have a refined sixth-sense about such things."

Lindsey rolled her eyes. Stewart could barely get dressed by himself in the morning. Nine times out of ten, he'd walk out the front door with his fly down if she didn't tell him to zip up, but she allowed him to live in his delusional world.

"Try to follow me here, Linds. First of all, he dresses like an extra from *Grease*. Combine with that the fake accent and oiled hair, and there's no way he doesn't play for the other team."

"Ummmm, well…" She covered her mouth to stifle another round of laughter. "You think his accent is fake?"

Dios narrowed his eyes and scowled.

Stewart continued, "Well, not completely. But it is much thicker than Cindie's, so I'm sure he's playing it up. I'll bet *those types* of guys think that's hot."

Lindsey shook her head. *Idiot.* "You do know people,

don't you? You may be right, but I think I can sell it. What husband would mind having a gay handyman help his wife out while he's away at the office?"

Dios bolted upright as though someone had pinched his butt. He pointed at himself and mouthed, "Gay?"

Stewart didn't say anything for a minute, and Lindsey gave him time to work it through. "True." Though he'd acquiesced, skepticism still tinged his voice. He would do it. The man lived to do the drone work that would drive others insane.

Lindsey smiled at her success. "So will you take care of it?"

"Seems like a waste of time and effort, but really I'm glad you're doing this. It's about time you did something with your life. I don't want you sitting around all day watching television anymore. It sets a bad example for the kids. And, to be honest, Cindie and I have been worried that all the recreational eating you've been doing will start catching up to you. She even has a couple of holistic weight loss books she wanted me to pass on to you. In spite of what you did to her Vespa, she only wants the best for you."

If Lindsey could have reached through the phone and punched him, she would have given him two black eyes and a bloody nose. *Dead. He just asked me to kill him. Put poison in his wine, a cobra in his briefcase, a bomb in his boxers. And I'm more than happy to oblige. I'll put both him and his slut girlfriend into the deepest darkest hole in North America.*

As if he hadn't done enough, he said, "Oh, one more thing."

After that last comment, I can't imagine what else there is to say. But with Stewart, there's always something. He couldn't just do something for someone without having his hand out expecting a payback.

She gritted her teeth. "Yes?"

"Since you're going to be his boss, seems like we should get some free labor out of it. Do a little bartering, okay? I'll keep a log of my hours and expenses to get him set up as your employee, and I'll let you work out what you think is fair. Tell him to do a good job and keep you satisfied."

Lindsey relaxed. "Oh, I think he'll be *up* for that. I'll talk to him. I'm sure he'll do whatever I ask. Thanks."

As soon as the call disconnected, she released a flurry of curses. Her anger flared white-hot. Lindsey turned toward Dios. "I'm your boss now, and I'm demanding some free labor. After what I just went through, you'd better be more than up to the task too."

He rolled on top of her and pinned her hands to the bed. "I think we can work something out." Kissing her lips then her chin, he worked his way down her neck to the hollow of her throat.

"So sexy," he murmured. He released her hands and slid his fingers down her torso.

She gripped his hair. "You need to keep me satisfied. Stewart said so." Her breath caught as he teased her full breasts, cooling her fury thermostat down while cranking up her hormonal one until her lady parts verged on shooting fire and fumes like an irate volcano. Finally, he gave her satisfaction, taking one nipple and then the other into his mouth. The party girl growled with satisfaction and triumph. *Genius. I'm a frigging genius. Oh, yeah. I think we can work something out, Stewie. Don't you worry about that.*

Then, as Dios' talented lips passed her navel, he drove all thoughts of the business, and Stewart, from her mind.

Dios and Lindsey celebrated long and hard throughout the remaining afternoon, but as their sweat evaporated and they dozed in her bed, guilt pitched a tent and stoked the fires of havoc in Dios' mind. He tried to stop the chaos raging through his mind, but he had no more success controlling his emotions than he did following a women's beach volleyball game. Distracted by bikini-clad butts and shapely thighs, he could not keep track of, nor capture, the ball of his thoughts. Unable to remain quiet, he poked Lindsey in the shoulder. "Hey, Linds?"

"Mmmmmmm?" She lay against his arm but didn't open her eyes.

"What we are doing…"

"What about it?"

He hesitated. "I've never had a wife."

She still hadn't moved but laughed low and quiet. "I know. That's what makes this so perfect."

"Don't get me wrong, I'm very grateful for everything you've taught me. But… Well, I guess what I'm wondering about is you, and my other…um…customers, shouldn't you be working on your marriages instead of looking for distractions and satisfaction outside of your relationships?"

Lindsey's eyes snapped open, and she popped up. Though the blankets fell from her bare shoulders, he didn't dare look. As her glare blazed down on him, hotter than Godzilla's breath after a plateful of jalapenos and a pint of gasoline, he averted his gaze for fear of turning to a Dios-shaped pile of ash. He'd just poked a sleeping monster, and now she loomed, casting a dark shadow over him. Pushing himself up to a sitting position, he propped against the headboard. He wanted to run like a terrified beagle, but he had nowhere to go.

She pressed her finger against his chest. "Are you applying to be my therapist? Because if that's the case, we need to end this now."

He shook his head. "No. No, I just thought…"

"You don't think." She emphasized each word with a thump against his sternum. "You have no idea what my life is like. My lifetime of servitude is hell, worse than any prison sentence you can imagine."

Dios' heart banged around as he held up his hands in surrender. "I'm sorry. I just wondered…"

"No!" Her cheeks flushed a bright shade of red that bordered on purple. "You don't wonder. Don't think. Don't ask questions. Anyone who hires you will be beyond worrying about cheating, Dios. They will have already talked about things ad nauseam—that's what our girlfriends are for—so don't ask. What they'll want from you is a little attention, a little flirting, a little conversation, and some of this." She reached down and cupped his testicles in a firm grip that galloped right past painful and into application-for-a-boy-choir range, but he didn't dare move away.

She sneered at him, narrowing her eyes with an intensity that almost gave him a sunburn. "So, my newest employee, would you rather *have* me on the couch pouring my heart out?" She began to move her fingers, rolling him and toying with him. "Or would you rather have me on the couch?"

All his former curiosity—and moral misgivings—vaporized as he concentrated on the motions of her hand. He gulped. "I…ummm…"

"Yessss?" She purred as she kissed the spot on his chest where she'd been pounding. Her lips brushed his ribs and then his stomach.

He plunged his hands into her hair. "My…um…job isn't to worry about such things. I'll just take care of my clients' needs."

"Good man." She set him free, relieving him of the burden of responsibility. It no longer weighed him down, no longer made him hesitate or ponder the right and wrong of what he did. If she, whomever he served at the time, had decided to be with him, the betrayal of her husband had nothing to do with him.

Chapter 8

Dios lay in bed staring at the ceiling of his apartment. The digital clock glared down on him like a red-eyed cyclops.

He rubbed the bruise on his breast bone while mentally replaying the morals conversation he'd had with Lindsey. Though he would never bring up the subject of cheating wives again, his imagination conjured up new horrors that could not only destroy their new business but also threaten both his life and freedom.

Stewart. Lindsey had set everything up assuming that her husband would never know anything. But if he discovered what they'd been doing and spread the word, the husbands of Dios' clients would storm his apartment with pitchforks and torches as though driving out the wolf man or a gang of vampires. He could have snapped Stewart's brittle, broomstick neck like a chicken bone, but he'd need the badass skills of Jackie Chan and Bruce Lee to fight off a mob hell-bent on hanging him from the town's flag pole.

A flame of anger burst in his heart. Just because he used his unrivaled good looks, charm, and suave to keep the neglected ladies of Alabaster Cove entertained during the long, lonely afternoons while their husbands did whatever they did didn't mean that he deserved to be persecuted. He had a right, same as anyone, to earn a living.

He flipped over, trying to rid himself of these images as they marched like soldiers through the war-torn land of his imagination. Lindsey had taught him discretion, and he had proven that he could keep his shit together. He'd eaten dinner with the Newman family and then claimed Lindsey in the bathroom after everyone else had gone upstairs. But he hated that anyone—least of all Stewart—thought he was gay. He longed to show the little priss just how not-gay he was by posting a video on the internet of him and Lindsey screwing in the accountant's own bed. Dios grinned at the image of the man's face turning red with shame, knowing he'd never be able to compete with someone so sexy and well-hung.

But he had to admit, thanks to Stewart believing him limp-wristed, he got full, easy access to Lindsey. He couldn't let what the husbands thought bother him. If he charmed and smiled, no one would ever suspect he was paid to make the ladies of The Cove moan and cry out in pleasure.

But no matter how he and Lindsey dressed this monkey—calling it "handyman services" or "male escort"—he'd become a gigolo, a male prostitute, a mimbo, and Lindsey his pimp. And even if he managed to avoid the revenge of the husbands, the police could catch him and throw him in the slammer. Lindsey had told him she'd "dealt" with the local law enforcement, though she hadn't explained how. If he did the long walk down Cellblock Aisle, the other men would whistle and call his name, each negotiating their latest boy toy's value. When he donned that jumpsuit—his dark complexion would be striking against bright orange—the inmates would auction off his virginal asshole to the highest bidder. His stomach roiled at the images of that first night in his new home as some tattooed—and very large—inmate's bitch.

Turning on to his back once again, he ran his hand underneath the thin sheet, tracing the defined muscles in his chest, his lean abs, and rock-hard thighs. A body like his would forever be in demand—both inside prison and out. Cursing under his breath, he wished he'd been born with brains and super ninja skills instead of just beauty.

Shaking, he buried his face in the pillow and groaned. His parents had escaped the wars in Peru to provide a better life for their only son. To end up in prison spat in the face of their dreams. Before he leapt out of bed to pack his bag and flee for the hills, Dios remembered that the local fuzz in the Cove supported a simpler, more relaxed set of rules than the corrupt government his family escaped. A little cash under the table and a joint or two a week ought to be enough to keep the police out of his business.

His shoulder muscles—and sphincter—relaxed as his fear of going to the pen faded and his mind focused on something else that had been bothering him.

He was the perfect male, lusted after by every female on the planet. He knew how to seduce and talk and keep his shit together. Given that, why work for someone else? Lindsey had the brains to come up with the idea, but that didn't give her the right to use him and take a cut of his hard-earned money.

Sure, he owed her a small something for all the training and advice but nothing more. He would decide on a fair amount and give it to her from his first few jobs.

Dios smiled as his plan came together. He'd call Lindsey first thing in the morning. She wouldn't be thrilled about it, but she'd see the logic behind what he said.

To flex his seduction and charm muscles, he needed to branch out, sample a variety of flavors, and exercise his newfound skills on someone besides Lindsey. He grinned as images of the hundreds of eligible women in town danced through his mind. Not that it was likely, but if he crashed and burned on the first one, he'd try again, and again, until he got it right.

He'd perfect his skills just as any good businessman would.

Since his new job required him to stay gorgeous and blemish-free, he pushed the unsettling thoughts from his mind and prepared to get his usual twelve hours of beauty sleep. Pulling the sheets up to his chin, Dios drifted off to dreams of making love to hundreds of women on beds made of tens and twenties.

Part 2

Chapter 9

Angel's mind drifted millions of miles from the mechanical motions of scanning groceries and asking the same inane, tired questions over and over. "How's your day going?"

A timid woman with graying hair said something, though Angel didn't listen to what.

"Uh huh." Suppressing a huge sigh that might have blown the small woman over, Angel continued to scan item after item with mindless monotony. The customers could have said they were headed to the hospital for a lung transplant or had just won the lottery, and her answer would have been the same. Uninteresting people with uninteresting lives fed her suicidal desires and homicidal tendencies. Blah blah blah.

The next customer set his groceries on the conveyor. Without looking up, Angel the automaton began running through her spiel. "How's your day going?"

"Good afternoon." The voice, deep silk with the hint of an unknown accent, stopped her cold. She glanced up. Captured by dark, sultry eyes, she remained frozen mid-scan as if she'd regressed to childhood and someone had yelled, "Simon says, 'Freeze!'"

Angel forced her hand to continue the swipe. The computer beeped. Then again. And again.

The man cocked his head. "How many times are you planning to charge me for my strawberries?" He smiled a little knowing grin, like they shared a private joke.

"Huh? Oh!" She dragged her gaze from his and began to fumble with the register. She pulled the ticker tape and tried to back out the extra transactions. Her fingers bumbled and tumbled over the little keypad. The computer, unamused with her antics, beeped again. The stern lecture from the machine only added to her fluster.

Hitting the clear key resulted in angry tweeps and twerps that echoed across the store. "Oh, you damned thing," she muttered. Embarrassed, with a large dollop of agitation to go with it, Angel swiped her badge over and over, her mortification giving way to desperation. The confounded contraption yowled like a nervous Chihuahua on espresso. Other customers as well as Jeff, the floor manager, stared.

"Mother effing, son of a bitch." She smacked the side of the computer, and the digital braying ceased.

Silence descended like a San Francisco fog on the front third of the store. Across the room, Jeff grimaced and shook his head. Angel reset the transaction, straightened her shirt, and took a deep breath. "I apologize; sometimes technology can be a little temperamental."

The man with the silky voice smiled as if she hadn't just made a total ass of herself. "Indeed, it can."

She drank in the tight t-shirt housing sculpted shoulders and a chiseled chest. His hair, thick and wavy and as black as raven feathers, complemented his warm and creamy, milk chocolate complexion. His black-quartz colored eyes sparkled with amusement.

She started scanning again while teetering on her tiptoes to peer over the check-writing counter. "They only give us a few hours of training, so when something goes wrong, we don't know what to do. It's really frustrating."

He chuckled. "I can well imagine."

Come on. Come up with something, anything besides the stupid cash register to talk about. "I like your jeans." *Oh my gawd. I just told him he looks hot in his pants. Too stupid to run a checkout line, and now I've just told him I'm checking out his assets. Could I be any dumber or more desperate?*

He moved past the little counter, held up his arms, and spun. "Thank you. I ordered them online from a place that does custom tailoring. You choose a style, then enter in your… what do you call them? Dimensions?"

She'd stopped scanning again and instead gawked like a school girl who had just met her favorite rock star. "Measurements."

"That's it. There is a tape you use that goes here." He pointed to his waist. "And here." He pointed to his crotch.

She licked her lips. "Your inseam."

His eyes lit up as his grin widened. "Oh, you know about sewing? My gran-mama used to make amazing traditional Peruvian clothes. It's a dying art." When he leaned over the check-writing counter, she caught a whiff of his cologne. He lowered his voice, and she bent closer to hear. "Maybe the next time I need new measurements, you would be willing to come and do them for me?" He winked.

It took every ounce of self-control for Angel to keep from drooling. "I…umm…would be happy to."

"Very good. I will come by soon." He handed her some money and left with his groceries. Her gaze lingered on his physique and casual gait until he'd disappeared from sight. She wiped her forehead, expecting it to be hot and sweaty. To her surprise, her hand came away dry, even though it seemed like someone had cranked up the temperature of the store to someplace between Sahara and molten.

The next person in line cleared her throat. "Uhhh hummm."

Angel glanced up. "Oh…um…sorry." She began processing the next batch of items on the belt.

The woman followed Angel's gaze to where the silky-voiced man had left. "He is gorgeous and charming."

Angel didn't respond. Instead, she blew out a long breath and fanned a hand in front of her face, trying to create a bit of a breeze.

The customer tapped her cheek with a manicured nail, an impish grin playing across her frosty pink lips. "You know, when you have someone like that come through your aisle and you're interested in getting to know him, you may want to try a clean shirt and a dab of makeup. You're a pretty girl; show him that."

Angel studied the dark-haired woman with the vibrant green eyes. Petite, athletic, and stunning in a non-assuming way. Her customer smiled wider. Angel sighed. *You are the kind of girl someone like him goes for. He'd never give me a second thought.*

The woman took her bag and turned back to Angel. "He will like you. Just show him who you are, and he'll be putty in your hands."

No one else waited in line, so Angel reached up and flipped a small switch. The check stand light went dark with a sharp *snick.*

"I'm going on break, Jeff," she said to the floor manager. Without waiting for a reply, she strode to the bathroom, pushed through the door, and examined her reflection in the mirror.

She sported a haphazard ponytail and no makeup. Fortunately, her clear skin didn't need much. Her shirt, wrinkled and two sizes too large, gave her a little-girl-dressing-in-daddy's-clothes look. Her frumpy chinos and stained apron completed the out-of-tune ensemble.

Yep, you're ready for your Paris runway debut.

She righted her ponytail with a hard yank and tucked in her shirt. But without one of those TV makeover teams, she wouldn't even be ready for an abandoned airport runway debut.

Heading back out on the floor, Angel made a beeline for the little man with the clipboard. "Jeff, I need to go home."

He frowned and scanned the schedule. "You're only half through your shift, and we're already shorthanded."

"I know, but I don't feel well."

He sighed. "What is it? Stomach or something?"

She grimaced. "Female problems." *Close enough.*

Jeff held up his hands and stepped away from her as if she'd just revealed she suffered from the plague. "Okay, okay. Go clock out."

The small pile of mail in the entryway scattered like leaves in a hurricane as Angel flew through the front door of her apartment. She slipped on one of the travel magazines delivered that afternoon and, without breaking stride, scooped it up and tossed it on the pile next to the easy chair. Angel continued her march to the bathroom where she took a long shower, taking care to soap her hair and lather herself with scented body wash. Leaving a trail of water in her wake, she got out and dug under the counter until she found the unopened package of razors. Cardboard and plastic flew as she ripped it open and yanked out one of the pink handles with a detachable head. Oblivious to the pending flood in her bathroom, she returned to the scalding spray.

Thirty minutes later, Angel stood in her closet, clad only in her underwear, with her hair wrapped in a towel. She pulled some shirts and slacks off the rod but tossed each piece aside. Most of her wardrobe looked like it had been stolen from a homeless shelter. After a short while, she'd thrown everything onto the floor. She ruffled her still-damp hair and kicked the pathetic pile with a frustrated grunt.

Since a couple of hours remained before the stores closed, she slipped on some sweats and headed out into the bright afternoon sunshine, driving her battered Beetle toward town and, hopefully, a new Angel.

The next day, Angel walked into the market to start her shift. Jeff glanced at her then down at his clipboard. A second later, his head snapped back up as if someone had grabbed his pathetic little rat tail and yanked.

Sexual harassment rules terrified him—he had gone on and on and on at the last employee meeting about never making comments or flirting with other employees—so he didn't say anything. But he didn't need to. His wide eyes spoke the words his mouth could not as he scanned from her curled hair all the way down to her new brown boots. She held her head high as she allowed him to ogle her pressed slacks and fitted shirt.

"Register three is ready for you." His eyes lingered on her figure.

She smiled, patted his head, and started towards her booth. "Thank you, Jeff."

During the mid-morning rush, the usual stay-at-homes came through to get their daily supply of diapers, baby food, and celebrity magazines. Energized in a way she hadn't been in years, Angel started conversations with these bored, longing-for-adult-human-interaction housewives. She made it her job to help break up the monotony of daytime soap operas and spilled cereal by engaging in pleasant small town chitchat. She had a career—so to speak—and spent her days meeting people, but soon she would be on a path to something bigger and greater. In the past few months, she'd stepped up her travel magazine research as she waited for that grand day when her plans to have plans solidified into an actual blueprint for her future.

The morning flew by, and she loathed leaving when Jeff told her to go to lunch. She'd unlatched the top few buttons of her blouse and batted her eyes in hopes of swaying him to do her bidding. But he'd held up his hand and cited some inane regulation, though something pressed hard against the front of his pants, as obvious as a buoy in the middle of the flat ocean. Little did Jeff know, he and his "regulations" might very well prevent Angel from fulfilling her destiny. He and his puny pant-bulge could cockblock her potential date with the dark-haired demigod.

Without any other options, she sighed loudly enough for the manager to hear clear across the room, forced herself to snap off the register's light, and trudged towards the second-story break room where she'd be able to monitor the entire store. She sat on the hard plastic bench, lording over all below, her gaze darting from customer to customer. Angel's heart stopped as she zoomed in, focusing sniper-like on a single point.

Dark hair. Milk chocolate skin. Defined shoulders. Tight jeans. *Clean-up in the produce department!* As if Zeus himself had come down from Mount Olympus on a golden chariot to recharge his master bolt with the grocery's fine selection of kumquats and corn on the cob, he surveyed the assortment of fruits and vegetables.

She sailed down the stairs and out onto the floor where she speed-walked her way to the produce department and her Zeus.

Chapter 10

Angel crossed the store in world record time. The closer she got to him, the more her eyes fondled his glorious manscape. The dark-haired deity looked even better today than she remembered from yesterday. Since she'd seen him last, he'd grown into the mythical king of the gods. How could he have possibly gotten more handsome in such a short span?

She entered the department and checked her cadence, acting as casual as her jazzed nerves allowed. *Not doing anything here, just picking out something to eat for my snack.* Zeus examined a bunch of bananas, shook his head, put them back, and picked up some more.

Sidling up next to the table, she looked the bunch over with mock disgust. "The guy who puts these out doesn't have any idea how to be gentle and bruises the hell out of them. If you want, I can get you some from the back that don't look as if they've been in a brawl."

He glanced up and smiled. "Fruit is very tendar and needs to be handled as such."

Her girl thermostat climbed as his smooth, melodious accent washed over her. If he continued to talk to her, she might just melt into her boots and puddle all over the floor as though her body had been made of chocolate and left out in the sun.

Placing the bunch back onto the table, he turned to her and leaned against the fruit. "If you'd be willing to pick me out something that has a touch of green and no black, I'd owe you a favor."

He could have made a request for her to fly to the moon and bring him back a dab of green cheese, and she would have asked if he wanted it shredded or in a block. She licked her lips, envious of the banana trapped beneath his butt, and held up a finger. "Be right back." She flittered off toward the far wall of the department.

He would owe her... Oh. My. Gawd.

She barreled into the entrance of the produce cooler. The dragging whoosh-floop of the heavy swinging doors echoed throughout the frigid storage chamber. A cool breeze dampened and chilled her skin as though a giant yeti had run its icy tongue up and down his favorite Angel-flavored Popsicle.

At the immediate front of the large space stood a huge table like an Aztecan alter—its wooden surface pocked with thousands of cuts, stained from the juices of a never-ending queue of fruit offered up in sacrifice. She wandered deeper, inspecting pallets full of haphazardly placed crates. Angel had never paid attention to the goings-on elsewhere in the store, so she didn't know how to find anything.

Maybe she wouldn't be able to fulfill her promise after all. She spun like a miswired merry-go-round until her gaze landed on a pile of boxes marked "Chiquita."

She lifted the lid off the closest box, rummaged through it until she found just the right bunch and, carrying the fruit like a victory banner, headed to the front of the cooler. Her good spirits faded though as doubt crept in. Maybe she'd taken too long and the man with the silky voice had grown tired of waiting.

Angel sprinted, hitting the big swinging doors with

her shoulder and muscling them open. She scanned the department then released a pent up breath. Zeus still leaned against the table, gazing through the outside wall of glass, as though he'd posed for a sculptor. The resulting statue would have rivaled the physique of Atlas in Rockefeller Center in New York.

She started to run, caught herself, speed-walked, started running again, and slowed yet again—resulting in a spastic gait that would have made a stumbling drunk on an out of control Tilt-O-Whirl look graceful.

When she reached him, she presented the bananas like a prized hog at the county fair, complete with a big, cheesy grin to go along with it. "Here you go."

He turned and smiled. When he accepted the fruit, his fingers grazed hers. A spark zipped up her arm and traversed the length of her body, a mild but pleasant wave of electricity. He allowed their touch to linger for a heartbeat before breaking contact and putting the bundle in the basket at his feet. "Thank you."

She could not tear her gaze from his. "Oh, it's no problem."

He cocked his head. "I've seen you before." He snapped his fingers. "You were running the cash register yesterday afternoon." He looked her up and down. "You seem… different."

Oh, shit. Why? Why didn't I look good yesterday? "Yeah, I wasn't feeling well, and by the end of the day, I was looking a bit rough. Doing *a lot* better today."

Her stomach lurched, and her cheeks burned as she lied to this man-god. If he saw through her ruse, he'd summon the air and ride off on a lightning bolt to places unknown. But if she pulled it off, she could be one of the lucky women chosen to consort with an immortal. Swallowing hard, she managed to slip him her best flirty smile.

In response, his lips turned up into a grin. She stood as still

as an oak in the dead of winter, mesmerized by him. The smile
had transformed him from rogue handsome into dashing. She
thanked the Titans for producing such an awe-inspiring piece
of ass…art.

He placed his hand on her lower back. "Well, I am sorry
to hear that, but I'm glad you are doing better. I must say the
difference is remarkable."

She twirled. "You like?" *Seriously? You are spinning around
like a thirteen-year-old. Have some dignity, woman.*

He tipped his head and nodded in approval. "Oh, very
much."

Ha! He did it for me yesterday, so I can do it for him today.
She offered her hand. "I'm Angel."

He took it in his own. But, instead of shaking it, he bent at
the waist and, watching her, pressed his lips to the back of it.
"I'll bet you are an angel. My name is Emigdio, but you may
call me Dios."

Her breath caught, and her heart stopped. This hand-kiss
come-on, so absurd and cheesy and centuries out-of-date,
shouldn't have worked, but when Zeus' warm breath caressed
her skin, tendrils of heat flooded her body and tantalized her
nerve endings.

Their conversation continued, though her mind lingered on
the way he'd looked at her, the gentle way he'd held her hand,
and the softness of his lips on her skin. *Hmmmm wonder what
his lips would feel like on other parts of my body?* A shudder tore
through her.

"…so why don't you come over for dinnar? You'd be the
first guest in my new home. My place is…"

Her mind snapped back into the conversation. "Huh?
What?"

Zeus examined her for a moment, concern flickering
through those hypnotic eyes. "Are you sure you're okay?
Maybe yesterday's illness still has a hold on you."

Angel shook her head. "What? No! I'm fine." She touched his arm and softened her voice. "Thank you for worrying about me."

Hey, Dufus! Pay attention! He just asked you out but you're so busy thinking about being ravaged by a god that you almost missed it.

Well, excuse me! It's been a little while since…well, since anything has ever happened that I got a little caught up in the moment.

Okay, fine, but give him your number and even more importantly: pay attention!

She dropped her hand to his and squeezed. "So you were saying something about dinnar…er, dinner?"

He smiled again, further flummoxing her overloaded, hormone-infused mind. "Tonight, after your shift is done, come over, and I'll cook you a traditional meal like granmama used to make."

She rummaged through her apron pocket. Finding a mangy scrap of paper, she wrote her number and handed it to him with quaking fingers.

He chuckled. "This is a yes then?"

Her head bobbed like a rubber duck in the water. "I get done at seven."

Zeus wrote his address on the back of a card and tucked it into the breast pocket of her apron. Taking her hand, he kissed it again. "It has been very nice to meet you, Angel. I look forward to seeing more of you tonight." He smiled one last time before he strode away.

Za-zing. I'm sleepin' with this guy. No. Doubt. About. It.

"Angel to register three." In some other universe, a voice dive-bombed her.

Though summoned, she refused to pry her eyes off him until the automatic door slid into place and blocked her view. Even when he'd disappeared, she remained riveted to her spot, in awe.

Zeus—her Zeus. *Hers!*—would cook for her tonight. He

would smile and press his lips to her hand and say exotic things like "dinnar" and "tendar." And the way he'd look at her right before they kissed…

She closed her eyes.

"Angel!"

Slap-startled awake, she spun on the intruder into her daydream. "Jeff? What, Jeff? Gawd. What do you need?" With her hands on her hips, she glared at him.

He stepped back. "I've been calling you over the intercom. Your break is done, and I need you on register three."

She blinked several times and shook her head to clear away the sound of the angelic choir singing the "Hallelujah Chorus" in her mind. "Huh? Oh, okay."

Jeff turned to leave but stopped himself. He leaned in closer to examine her face. "You're flushed and breathing hard like you just ran a marathon or something. Are you okay?"

She gave him a sly half-grin. "Oh, I'm more than okay."

He hesitated, frowning, but then trundled away.

She took a huge breath and spun to follow when her foot kicked something hard. As she stumbled to right herself, she noticed the basket of groceries Zeus had been collecting—the bunch of bananas perched on top. She examined the bundle for a moment, turned, and floated toward her register.

He hadn't even come for the groceries. Which meant he'd made a special trip to see her. She covered her mouth and released a muffled squeal before returning to the mindlessness of her pre-Zeus life.

Chapter 11

As the rest of the afternoon dragged on, Angel checked her watch every few minutes, willing the time to move faster. When the glacial hands on the clock clicked to seven, she bolted from behind her register and flew out the door, tossing a goodbye to Jeff along the way.

At home, she showered and put on the new Victoria's Secret panties and matching push-up bra she had purchased the day before. *God bless the R&D scientists at Vickies. Flat-chested girls the world over worship the ground you walk on.*

She slipped into her best form-fitting red dress, which showed off the mild curves of her petite body and the newly formed cleavage created by the expensive underwear. A matching red headband in her short, dishwater blonde hair and conservative black, low open-toed heels completed the package.

Dark red against creamy, white, pale skin. Yin and Yang. She smiled at the reflection in the mirror. *Not bad! Not bad at all!* But as she slammed the door on her battered Beetle, and began ascending the stairs to his condo, she fidgeted with her slinky short dress, which rose with every step. Maybe she'd crossed the subtle line between provocative and desperate. At home, her outfit had screamed "come get me big boy," but now it flashed like a red light on Whore St. She considered turning around and running back to her apartment where she'd shed the "two dollar hooker" garment and opt for jeans and a simple t-shirt instead. Though the tight denim would show off her I-never-quite-fully-developed-boobies-and-curves figure, a snug pair of jeans could also be… inconvenient when…if she needed a no-fuss, no-muss way to take them off.

She argued with herself about what to do all the way up the walk to his front door, yanking down her dress every time it began its northern migration. Pausing one last time to adjust her assets, she pushed the little glowing doorbell and surrendered her wardrobe to the fates.

From beyond the entrance, footsteps approached. She popped open her makeup mirror, glancing in it to make sure she didn't have a booger or something else embarrassing hanging from her nose. As the handle twisted, she snapped the mirror shut and slipped it into her purse.

Dios opened the door and greeted her Zeus-like—bare feet, dark colored slacks, and an untucked white shirt, which made his creamy-chocolate skin glow. When he flashed her an easy smile, she relaxed. Then his dark eyes scanned her body, pausing at the deep V of her dress before returning to her face.

Give those scientists at Vickies a raise, please! Her mental conductor tapped his wand on the music stand, raised it up, and the choir of cherubs once again began singing the "Hallelujah Chorus" while a ray of pure light shone down around her deity on Earth.

When he took her hand and led her inside, she willed her wobbly legs to follow along and not send her spilling to the floor like a newborn calf. He paused in the entryway, motioning to a pair of aged sandals beside the door. She nodded—*must be some of that feng shui crap*—removed her conservative black heels, and placed them beside the well-loved leather.

Yin and yang. There's a good chance I won't be putting those back on until tomorrow.

He guided her further into the house and the most wonderful aroma of sautéed onions, garlic, and frying meat enveloped her. As she entered the living room, the visual stimuli joined the olfactory-gasm creating a sensory overload that threatened to leave her gasping.

Spinning in a slow circle, she marveled at the coordinated furniture and tasteful prints decorating the comfortable space. "Wow, nice place."

He gave her a sly smile. "Not what you expected, no?" His silky voice and harmonizing accent played like a symphony to her ears.

She shook her head but didn't say anything.

He handed her a goblet of wine—the burgundy liquid shimmered and glowed in the low light—while he did that thing again, where he imprisoned her eyes with his. After he clinked his glass with hers, she took a sip. She'd only ever had on-sale booze in a box, so the velvety richness of the elixir danced and pirouetted across her tongue and took her breath away. *Zeus in a Cup. That's what I've got. This beautiful, intoxicating man, liquefied himself and poured me a glass.*

Dios leaned toward her. His kiss—sensual without being overtly sexual, lips firm but gentle—seized Angel's synapses. Cascading waves of heat, like warm honey, rippled and weaved their way through every fiber in her body.

As their breaths mixed, a little sweetness from the wine made an encore appearance tantalizing her taste buds anew. He looked into her eyes, and a deep, carnal part lusted to offer herself on the altar of this new-found sex god.

He smiled that sly grin of his and winked. "Dinnar will be ready in a moment. Please, make yourself comfortable while

I finish up." Though her mind remained jammed, her heart thrummed as quickly as a hummingbird's wings. Like a hungry puppy, she padded along behind him to the kitchen.

On the stove, several pans simmered. Wonderful smells emanated from their depths. He lowered the temperature of the burners and stirred a red sauce with a wooden spoon, tasted it, took a pinch of some spice from a small bowl, and sprinkled it across the bubbling surface of the thick liquid.

He offered the spoon to her, which became a sextensil in his hands.

When she tasted the rich red sauce, her eyes rolled back in pleasure. "It's amazing. What is it?"

He continued to stir the pot. "Family recipe from the old country, handed down from my great-grandmother whose meals were the subject of legend." He waved at the various pots. "None of this is written down, you know. Food is about both tradition and marking the world by making a recipe your own. I like things a little spicier than gran-mama did." He held her eyes. "I like my meals to be very sensual but still have a little zing."

Her mind had been beaten and lay gasping against the ropes. She gave in to her feral, primal instincts and did what her body commanded her to do. She kissed him, gently at first, and then she crushed her lips against his as though to consume him.

Breaking their kiss, he turned off the burners and took the wine from her hand. He wrapped a muscular arm around her shoulders and, with the other arm under her knees, picked her up and carried her to the bedroom, kissing her as he walked.

The soft light of half a dozen candles illuminated the lavish space. He continued to kiss her while he laid her on the soft bed. She gazed up at his face. The very air around him flickered and flashed, the flames inspired to dance by their union.

Zeus didn't talk much, but what his tongue lacked in verbal use, it more than made up for in other ways. The maestro took his time lavishing her, strumming her body like the finest of instruments. He knew the right places to touch, stroke, and kiss as if he had a special Angel-edition AAA roadmap.

She didn't know him but understood and connected with him on an emotional level that escaped definition. His performance proved to be flawless, beyond anything she'd expected or experienced.

After the curtain came down and he fell asleep, she snuck out, climbed into her dilapidated Beetle, and got to bed only two hours before having to be back up for her next shift at the market.

Yawning her way through the day, Angel's mind remained back in Dios' apartment. The glow in his eyes. The firmness of his body. The perfect movements of his fingers, lips, and hips.

But something about him and their evening together left an acted-out, performing taste in her mouth. She couldn't put her finger on what tripped her suspicions, just a feeling. An offness.

In spite of misgivings, her hormonal, love-starved body screamed for more and doused the logical, rational part of her that knew their…relationship…would implode in a ball of furious heat like a collapsing sun.

She had life plans…well, she had plans to have plans at least. At some undefined time in the future, she would kick the sand of this little town off her feet and move on to bigger and better things. Though *what* and *where* those things were, she didn't know. At least not yet. But whatever they turned out to be, they wouldn't involve a Greek love god.

But the sex had been so mind-blowing that she decided to take a gamble. She dialed him during her lunch break. "Hey, it's me."

"Hello to you."

They were better off as friends. She would make the hard choice for them both, and he would appreciate her honesty. "How would you feel about being friends with benefits?"

"I don't understand this term—friends with benefits. What does it mean?" His words rang with curiosity, and his velvet-smooth voice soothed her misgivings.

"It's where we stay friends, nothing more. Not boyfriend-girlfriend. Not tied down. I want to be friends that hangout together and screw. I won't ever stay at your place for the night. That's what people who are in a committed relationship do. I'll go home. It'll be strictly sexual." Then she remembered the good smells emanating from his kitchen. "Okay, maybe you could make me dinner too."

He remained quiet for a moment. "Yes. Okay, we can do this, if that is what you wish."

She breathed a sigh of relief. "It is. So, ummm, what are you doing tonight?"

A month later, while her Peruvian demi-god slumbered, Angel lay warm and safe in Dios' arms. During their time together—the weekends and evenings spent watching TV and screwing—he'd managed to wiggle into her heart. He'd done more than become part of her routine; he'd created an emotional warm spot. The concept of commitment terrified her—her luck in men had always ranged from poor to awful—but maybe the time had come to move things to the next level.

She'd never envisioned herself settling down with someone

like Dios. For all of his charm and worldly, deity-like appeal, they didn't have much to talk about. He watched a lot of movies and spent an inordinate amount of time at the gym. He also didn't have a job—nor had he been searching for one. So, she had no idea how he made money. But every relationship had its flaws, each party made their own concessions for the greater good. She could overlook these chinks in his otherwise perfect armor.

With her ear pressed to his chest, the slow and steady lub-dub of his heartbeat offered comforting reassurance. She could devote herself to just one man. She could make him part of her plans to have plans. She might even be able to love him.

Angel smiled. She burrowed deep beneath the covers, snuggling her body against his, and went to sleep.

Dios awoke with a start. He glanced at the nightstand clock—two in the morning—then lay there staring at the ceiling. Beside him, Angel's rhythmic and gentle snoring blared like a five-alarm fire bell in his head. He thought he'd been using her to further his skills as a lover and seducer, but somehow she'd snagged him into relationship hell. She came over every evening, texted him during the day, made plans for them on the weekends, and now she had escalated the situation by staying the night. And he had no idea how to get out of it. None.

Desperate, he untangled himself from the sleeping woman, crept down the hall to the spare bedroom, and closed the door. He loathed making the call but had no choice.

The phone rang in his ear, and he wondered if she'd even pick up. Maybe he'd pissed her off so much that she'd just laugh and leave him to deal with the mess on his own. But just when he thought it would go to voicemail, the call connected.

"Hello, Dios. I've been expecting you." Lindsey's voice carried an air of smug triumph over the wire.

He frowned, his relief at hearing her voice overshadowed by the surprise of her words. "You have?" He whisper-spoke for fear of talking too loudly and waking Angel up.

A light chuckle echoed through the earpiece. "It was just a matter of time before you got yourself in trouble. It's almost two AM, so let me guess. You've got a girl there, and she's just decided that you're boyfriend material and won't leave you alone."

He sucked in a sharp breath as his mind raced. *Could she be spying on me?* It seemed unlikely, stuff from movies, but still. "How did you know?"

"Because, you idiot, we never got to that part of your training. I told you when you decided to go out on your own that you couldn't do it without me. And here you are calling me in the middle of the night."

He shook his head, trying to follow her. No matter how hard he tried, Lindsey always seemed to be several steps ahead of him. "Yeah, yeah. Okay, fine. You win. I need your help. What do I do?"

"Hold on there, Elvis. You may be a hunka hunka burnin' love, but it doesn't work like that."

He sighed; time to eat some crow. "What? Do you want me to admit I was wrong? Fine. I was wrong."

"And?"

He rolled his eyes. "And you were right."

"That's better. From now on, if you ever question anything I tell you, I want you to repeat that little mantra over and over. Paste it on your social media page. Get it tattooed on your forehead. Now, let me hear it once more so I know you've got it."

He gritted his teeth. "I was wrong, and you were right."

Her voice purred. "Good, but there's something else."

She'd accused Stewart of never doing anything without extending his hand for some kind of payout, and here she was doing the same thing. "Okay, now what?"

"Now you agree to come back and work for me. You also have to agree that you'll never, ever pull another stunt like leaving again. Do I have your word?"

Exasperation, and an odd relief, flooded his veins. He could seduce and charm, but he needed Lindsey. Though it bruised his ego to admit, it had been a mistake to leave; he saw the truth of that now. "Yes. I agree. Now what do I do?"

Her cat-like smile carried in her voice. "Good man. Okay, time to solve your problem. Listen carefully."

Dios listened carefully, and his smile grew with each passing word.

As Angel cracked open her eyes, she had to hold up her hand to block the blazing sun shining through the bedroom window. Dios stood over her, holding a tray with a big cheesy grin on his lips.

He set the tray on her lap. "Good morning, honey!"

Still foggy from sleep, she tried to sit up and return his smile, but the expression faltered when she took in the meal he'd placed before her: limp, undercooked bacon and blackened toast with a side of burnt eggs. Not just overcooked like her mom would sometimes make, but scorched and inedible. Even the garnishing daisy had a wilted, depressed demeanor, as if embarrassed about the sad state of food he'd presented. To round out the ensemble, he'd brought her watery orange juice in a glass. A dirty glass.

This is a dream. You're still asleep, and at any second your lovely Zeus will be there beside you. Beautiful and perfect.

But when she pinched herself, it hurt, and her world didn't morph into the reality she knew and loved. She stared at the cup in her hand. "This glass isn't clean."

He laughed and shrugged. "Sorry. I've been meaning to have the guy come look at the dishwasher."

She stabbed a charcoaled egg. It broke into two pieces while black flakes fluttered across her plate and onto her lap.

Dios laughed again. "You've always been gone in the morning before I get up. Dinnar is no problem, but somehow, the morning meal always stumps me. I guess gran-mama didn't have any recipes for eggs."

He took her hand and tipped up her chin so they stared into one another's eyes. "We spend almost all of our time together. You come over every night, and I see you on the weekends."

She nodded and smiled. "Yeah, I've been thinking about that too."

He returned her smile. "So, I've been thinking, my parents are back in Peru, and I would love for them to meet you. Mamã has been nagging me to find a nice girl and settle down…in my home country."

The smile slid off her face as though it had been coated in oil. She reeled back, incredulous. "You…you want to take me home to meet your parents?" Her mind spun.

He touched her cheek and interlaced their fingers. "Well, it was so special to me that you decided to stay the night. I can tell that you also know it's time to take things to the next level."

She snatched her hand back. "Wait, that usually means dating exclusively, not moving to another country."

He touched her leg through the sheet and earnestness graced his eyes. "Since you are from America, Papa will forgo the usual expectation that your family will give him cows and sheep as a dowry. Unless your momma wants to. Do you think she'd want to honor our customs? If she moved with us, it would be expected of her." He looked off as in deep thought. "It might be easier for her to buy livestock in Peru instead of having them shipped over."

Her already-spinning mind now reeled, not sure what to focus on first. Cows and sheep. A future with him. Kids and a house…in Peru, so maybe a hut. Living in a strange village with her mom and his parents, where she didn't know the people or the customs. Maybe they wouldn't even have internet access or cable TV. Their friends' wives would, of course, flirt with her beautiful, charming Zeus at dinner parties while she walked around on a dirt floor, pregnant. Her boyfriend-thoughts of him burst like a thread-bare tire on hot asphalt.

She took a deep breath. Things had been clean and simple before she met Dios, but the more time she spent with him, the dirtier, more complicated her life became. Now he wanted to take her to Peru in exchange for cows and sheep?

Her phone on the nightstand buzzed. Angel held up a finger. "Hold that thought." *Or don't.*

Dios nodded, a happy, dopey smile returning to his face.

She picked up the phone and examined the caller ID. She didn't recognize the number but didn't care. Without a single idea who might be on the other end, she flipped open the little electronic savior. "Hello."

"Ang, it's me."

Though she hadn't heard the voice in months, she would have recognized her best friend, Monica, anywhere. "Mon! Oh my god! How are you?"

The three words her friend had spoken replayed themselves through her mind. The short crisp sentence, the staccato cadence, and the anxiety mingled…her friend needed help. "Wait, what's the matter? You said you weren't supposed to call me, and I don't recognize this number. What happened?"

Her friend's surprised voice came back. "Jesus, Ang, how do you do that?"

Angel shook her head. "It's a gift. Now spill." She got up and started to get dressed as Monica began speaking.

"I need your help…"

As Dios watched from his position on the bed, Angel slipped on her underwear and stuffed various items in her purse. Curiosity and concern shaped the beautiful features of the man's face. Angel made a writing motion with her hand, and Dios handed her a pad of paper and a pen.

She scratched out the address her friend rattled off. "Okay, hon." Angel checked her watch. "I should be there in a couple of hours."

She snapped the phone shut and turned to Dios. "I need to go."

He smiled. "So it seems. It sounds like your friend is in trouble."

"Also, since I'm going anyway, the whole Peru thing." She shook her head. "Yeah, that's never going to happen. In fact, we're done now."

His face fell. "Well, if that is the way you want it, then I will honor your wishes."

"It is. It really is." She kissed him on the cheek. "Bye, Dios. It's been fun."

He reached down to the floor at the foot of the bed and picked up a box. "Here are your things. I took the liberty of gathering them for you."

Startled, she almost dropped the box. "Um okay. Thanks. I appreciate it."

He walked over to the door and held it open for her. "Thank you, Angel. It's been a pleasure."

She moved toward the exit, not sure when it had turned from her leaving to him escorting her out. Well, it didn't matter, the end result would be the same. She paused just before crossing the threshold and smiled. "See ya."

"Adiós." He smiled back at her and began to close the door before she'd finished going through it.

She hurried out onto the porch as the door *snicked* shut and literally hit her in the ass. She'd had plans to have plans forever. The breakup of her relationship and the plea of her friend to come help could be a wakeup call from the universe telling her the time had come to make those plans. She needed to get on with her life. Quit her loser job, get out of the mangy apartment, and do something bigger than dead-end boyfriends and *Wheel of Fortune* by herself every evening.

Angel raced home, got a few traveling items from her apartment, and hit the road, bound for parts—and a future—unknown.

Chapter 12

Dios smiled as he watched the girl stumble from his apartment. His mother always said the devil lived in the details. A Peruvian dowry and the dirty glass had been genius. Mamã would have gone ballistic had they shown up at her apartment in Lima with livestock.

Angel said she'd only wanted to be "friends with benefits," and that arrangement had been fine for a while. But not even Angel could keep her distance while giving herself to him over and over. During their early morning conversation, Lindsey had explained how to make sure his unwanted guest bolted, and the hasty plan had worked better than Dios could have dreamed.

Angel had proven to be a complete idiot, with no aspirations—what the hell did "plans to have plans" mean exactly?—and no money. And because of that, she'd failed to hold his interest. She'd only been a test client, picked at random, used to bolster his confidence and perfect his performance. He now knew he could seduce anyone at any time; he would *never* do the pretend boyfriend thing again.

Like everything else, Lindsey had been spot on about that too. She'd warned him that setting out on his own would end in disaster.

And he didn't know if he'd do the cooking thing again

either. Maybe he could just burn a chocolate cookie candle rather than burning copious amounts of money on takeout. Buying the expensive meals had seemed like a good idea, and even though he'd gotten to eat the leftovers the next day, the cost made such a thing prohibitive and profit-sapping.

Dios could not make it on his own. He sighed. Lindsey had known this long before he had. They could only make it work…together.

Later that day, he visited Lindsey. Sitting side-by-side on stools in her kitchen, he examined his new business cards. His heart sank as he studied his picture on the light gray background. She'd known he would fail and had ordered business cards for him in advance. He never should have left. What an idiot he'd been to think he could make it on his own.

Lindsey flipped open a black, leather-bound book and tucked one of his cards into a plastic slot. Before she closed it, Dios stopped her.

He took the binder, flipped it back open, and stared, incredulous. The page had slots for ten business cards. Six of them contained pictures of men; their embossed names gleamed in raised lettering. "What's this?"

She smiled at him. "Those are my employees."

His mind sputtered. "Your employees? But…but…I…um…"

She turned and faced him full on. "You what? You left, remember? Did you think I was going to just sit around with my thumb up my ass and wait for you to come back?"

Dread, cold and hard, filled his gut. "No. I guess not."

"I'm a business woman, not a social worker. I didn't take it personally when you went off on your own to cut me out of the profits, so you can't feel cheated when I hire someone, or someones, to take your place."

He took a deep breath. "I suppose not. I'm sorry, Lindsey."

She looked at him a long time. "So there are still a couple of items to discuss. The first is that by pulling that little stunt, you've cost yourself a cut of the profits. Now, we're fifty-fifty."

Dios jumped to his feet; his stool clattered to the floor. "What? That's not fair."

Lindsey didn't react to his outburst. She just sat there, giving him a pitying expression he hated. "You don't have any choice. If it's any consolation, I may ask you to assist me in managing the other employees. If you do that, we might be able to renegotiate the terms. But until I'm sure I can trust you, it has to be this way. Now, next on the list: your apartment."

He cringed, already knowing what she would say. Righting the stool, he sat. "Yes?"

She squared her jaw and narrowed her eyes. "You got a loan from your aunt to redecorate it, didn't you? You don't have a source of income now that the coaching job is over, and I heard through the rumor mill that you bought some new furniture, wall prints, and so on."

"How did…"

She held up her hand. "Welcome to Mayberry circa nineteen fifty-five, Dios. Remember my lecture on discretion? Well, this is why. In a little town, all everyone has to talk about is each other."

He dropped his head. "Yes, I borrowed some money from Aunt Cindie. I thought I could pay her back. I bought food and wine and some other romantic stuff too."

Lindsey sighed. "I don't like my employees being in debt. It's a distraction and an unnecessary stress." She pursed her lips. "Send me the details of how much you got, what you spent it on, and how much you've got left. After that, forget about the loan. Consider it closed. Soon I'll have some negotiation leverage and will see to it that it's forgiven."

He furrowed his brows and looked at her. "Okay, but I don't understand. What do you mean you'll have leverage?"

She shook her head. "Never mind. It's just business. This obligation is no longer your problem, but don't ever borrow money again. From now on you'll run all expenses through me. Is that clear?"

He nodded. "Yes." Dios looked away, dejected. "What else?"

She reached up and touched his face. "Just so you know, I've not gone through the rigorous…training you and I did with any of my other employees. No one but you has touched me. That's just between us."

His heart leaped. "Really?"

She nodded. "In fact, I believe we still have a bartering agreement in place, and you owe me some free labor."

"I would never break our deal." He pushed the papers and dining paraphernalia out of the way. As the Newman family salt shaker rolled off the table and shattered on the floor, he picked her up, set her on the table, and covered her body in kisses.

Neither of them noticed the ruins of her dining room as they celebrated their reunion.

As they consummated their reunited business arrangement, Lindsey floated in a sea of pleasure and victory. Dios, her star pupil, would set the example for the rest of her employees. No one else would ever dare cross her because he'd see to their strict obedience better than a thousand lectures.

She needed him to keep the other men in line, which had
been the reason she'd let him leave in the first place. She
dangled the money carrot, making him believe that he had
what it took to make it on his own, only she'd kept a couple
of the key lessons to herself. After he'd called and broken off
their business arrangement, the clock had begun ticking on
when he'd beg her to help him clean up his mess and save
his well-shaped ass.

While Dios had learned some hard life lessons, she'd
found other willing, beautiful men to round out the roster
of her business venture. Two of these clods-turned-seducers
had already completed their training. Lindsey would begin
working with the next in a couple of days, rotating the men
through her school—and her bed—until they could handle
themselves.

The little white lie she'd told Dios had been nothing more
than a morale booster for her Peruvian protégé. He needed
to believe that, though she had many men in her employ, she
only had eyes for him. Each of her students had been told
something similar and had been sworn to secrecy. If they
feared her and didn't speak to one another, she should be
able to keep the troops in line and her sheets warm.

Also in his absence, she had constructed her marketing
plan. No matter how great her gigolos, without clients,
the business would fail. Her friends would help with that,
though they didn't know it yet. If the wrong people found
out, scandal would wreck her and pandemonium would
ensue. So they had to be careful whom they extended their
services to, but she had confidence that she'd picked the
right people for her marketing team.

That left one stone not yet dealt with: Stewart. He'd been
snooping around, poking in places he ought to have stayed
away from. After doing some nosing around of her own,
she'd found the evidence he'd been collecting in the back of

his desk drawer. She'd made photo copies of the lot and filed it with the other information she'd been gathering. The time for reckoning had come, and Stewie, her little man child, would wish he'd never heard of *New Man Handyman*.

Chapter 13

Lindsey sat on the couch, in the same place she'd waited for her husband after she'd bought the SUV. At a bit after six, his little, hot pink Fiat pulled up to the curb, and he raced through the rain into the house.

Stepping across the threshold, he brushed water from his coat onto the floor.

She sighed. "Please don't get my carpet wet."

He didn't reply but continued to shake out his umbrella, spraying droplets onto the wall, carpet, and couch.

Someone's feeling a bit smug today. Let's see what we can do about that.

Stewart hung his coat up and set his briefcase down. "I'm getting a beer. Do you want one?"

She motioned toward her tea. "I'm fine."

He smiled. "Suit yourself. But I'm guessing you're going to change your mind before long." He grabbed a brew from the fridge, popped the top, and plopped into the arm chair across from her.

She gave him a coquettish smile. "Have a good day at work?"

He smiled back. "It was fine. Got Jim's books in order finally. Had lunch at the club. Let's see, I think there was something else. Oh, yeah." He held up a finger. "I have some paperwork for your 'business.'" He did air quotes the same way the Elfin had the last time Lindsey had gone to their office.

She nodded. If she broke all of his fingers, he'd never be able to emphasize a word the same way again. But instead of snapping his bones, she let it go. "Thank you for taking care of that."

His smile grew as he popped the latches of his briefcase. Stewart pulled out a folder and tossed it onto the coffee table. It landed with a resounding thud in front of her.

Lindsey took a sip of her tea but made no move to retrieve the folder.

Stewart gave her a devious little smile. "Well, aren't you going to open it?" He looked like he'd placed a woopy cushion on her chair and asked her if she'd like to sit down.

She shook her head. "No, I trust everything is in order. You know how this stuff bores me."

He leaned forward, the devious smile turning into a smirk. "Oh, I don't think you'll find this boring. Not at all."

I've already looked at everything in your file, Stewie. It's a dry, uninteresting read, boring just like I told you. But if you want to go there, I'll play. She picked up the file, flipped it open, glanced inside, closed it, and set it on the couch.

He sat back, triumphant. "I know what you've been up to, Lindsey. The game is over, and you're going to jail. You're a madam. I've seen the pictures, and I think they're disgusting. The sex you're trafficking is men, not women, but you're still a pimp. I'm going to be contacting the sheriff, and he'll haul you off to prison. I'll divorce your ass, and because you're a felon, you won't get a dime. You'll get a court-appointed lawyer and twenty years." The gleam in his eyes and the jack-o-lantern smile belied his belief in his complete and utter victory. In his pathetic, puny little mind, nothing could take him down. Nothing could stop him.

She shook her head again. This would be his last moment of triumph before she crushed him like a scooter under her SUV's wheels. She didn't want it to end just yet. Give him a bit more rope to hang himself. "Seems like you've been doing your homework, Stewie."

He nodded. "Yep. I might not have pursued such extreme measures if you hadn't been such a bitch. But you ran over my girlfriend's Vespa and spent a bunch of money on that behemoth in the driveway. I'll sell it and get Cindie a nice new scooter, and then I'll invest the rest in the kids' school… after I buy myself some new golf clubs. I've grown kinda fond of the TV though. I think I'll keep that. The kids seem to like you, so maybe they'll make the drive up to the state pen to see you…on occasion." Finished with his gloating, Stewart reached for his cell phone.

She seethed. His false sense of self-righteousness had grated on her nerves for years. The time had come for his hypocritical blather to end. "Hold on a second, Stewie."

He laughed. "Don't think you can grovel your way out of this. I'm doing it. There will be no negotiations, no mercy." He picked up his phone and began to dial.

She'd sooner put him in the ground and spend the rest of her life in jail than beg for mercy. Lindsey let him press a few numbers before stopping him. "You may want to look at the other folder in your briefcase before you make that call."

His thumb stopped in midair, and the smile melted, just a little, from his lips. "Huh? What file?"

She and the party animal leaned forward. "The one at the very bottom, underneath all the other crap you haul around." The beast within her licked its chops in anticipation.

Doubt flickered through his eyes as Stewart set down his phone and rummaged around until he found the folder she'd slipped in that morning. He frowned and flipped it open. The transformation from smugness to incredulity to surprise to horror took only seconds. His face drained of all color, and his hands shook. "How…how…" He took a deep pull on the beer, spilling several drops on his tie.

Sitting back with her legs crossed, Lindsey set her tea on her knee and took a demure sip while the party animal slammed an imaginary football to the ground and did a touchdown dance. "See, you're not the only one that knows how to do research. You're a creature of habit, Stewart. Boring and pathetic. I know where you keep your 'secret' files. Your girlfriend is a Peruvian immigrant, who's been in my country a very long time, so I did a little digging of my own. Tell me, how long have you known she's here on an expired visa?"

"I…um…well…didn't know." He stammered but nothing coherent came out of his prissy little lips.

She tsked at him while the party animal shook its head. "Of course you did. Which is why you've been paying her under the table. According to the Federal Immigration and Nationality Act, harboring and assisting an illegal immigrant is punishable by up to five years in prison. You can take a look; I included a copy for you."

He made no move to open the file but slumped into his chair.

She took another sip of her tea. "Are you aware of the penalties for tax evasion and falsifying records to the IRS and the State of California?" She laughed. "Of course you are; you're a CPA."

He groaned. "Linds, I…"

She held up a finger to stop him. "And as for the other little matter of the sheriff. See, he and I are good friends who go way back to long before I met your sorry little ass. I stopped in the other day, and the two of us had a great chat. I know how things in this town work, so I took along a little something to help him…relax. He's a peace officer through and through. So, after explaining my little venture, he says that as long as no one gets hurt, the peace is maintained, and, of course, he gets a negligible cut of the profits. No harm, no foul." She frowned. "Though with the State of California and at least two federal agencies breathing down his neck should I go public with the Elfin situation, I don't think he'd be so understanding about the illegal immigrant issue. Maybe you should go ahead and call him to find out."

Her husband's face had gone ashen. "Who else has seen this? Who else knows?"

She studied him, trying to figure out what he'd do if she said no one else knew. Would he try and hurt her? She didn't believe he would, but then again she'd never envisioned her marriage devolving like it had. Fortunately, she'd never have to test his ability to control himself because she'd prepared for this question. "My lawyer has a set."

His eyes grew wide. "Your lawyer?"

"I also have other sets with others that I trust." She smirked. "You know, if anything ever happens to me."

"Oh, come on, Linds! Stop being so melodramatic; I'm not a murderer. I'd never hurt you."

She waggled a finger at him. "Now, now. I want you to think about what you planned for this afternoon. You were going to send me to jail, remember? I prevented you from calling the police. Had you done so, it wouldn't have worked out the way you thought, but you didn't know that. Let's see what else? Divorce me and make me use a court-appointed lawyer. Did I miss anything?"

He wiped a tear from his cheek. "I'm sorry."

Once, his tears may have elicited sympathy or sorrow. Instead their presence stoked the embers of her anger. The fury monster inside her roared in unison with the party animal. "Stop blubbering. You look like a little girl."

Stewart grimaced and wiped his nose with the sleeve of his jacket. He sat up straight and clasped his hands between his knees. "What do you want? Obviously you haven't yet turned me in or I'd be in cuffs and Cindie would be headed back to Peru."

She narrowed her eyes. She'd bitch slapped him into submission, and now she needed to press her advantage. "Well, first there's the matter of a small loan that your slut girlfriend made to her nephew."

He cocked his head, confusion written across his face. "What about it?"

"As of this minute, the debt is forgiven."

Stewart shook his head. "No, we can't do that. She can't afford it."

Lindsey sneered at him. "You don't understand. You aren't calling the shots here. I am. See, the Elfin can't afford not to."

He regarded her for a long time, and then he threw up his hands. "I guess I have no choice, do I?"

She leaned back. "Now you're starting to get it."

He blew out a long breath. "What else do you want?"

When Lindsey smiled, she could practically feel the devil horns knocking her halo aside. "To make your life a living hell."

Chapter 14

The next morning, Lindsey met her closest girlfriends—Savannah, Genie, and Polly—for coffee. After a few minutes of gossip-swapping, Lindsey took control of the conversation. "So ladies, you might be wondering why I called us all together."

With the exception of her new business venture, Lindsey had always been an open book. The women seated around the table knew of the trouble in her marriage, the cheating with Cindie Brady, and the whole mess.

Savannah flashed a triumphant smile and smacked the table with an open palm, the rings on her fingers clanking against the surface like thunder. "I think I know. And I think it's about damned time you left that bastard." Her eyes sparkled from beneath heavily painted lids as she looked around the table. "Seriously, have you heard the way he carries on with his assistant?" She turned her attention back to Lindsey. "Honestly, I don't know how you've managed to stay this long. I'd have kicked that asshole to the curb years ago."

Savannah picked up her coffee and held it in the air. "I raise my glass to the end of that pathetic excuse of a relationship and to the future ruination of a bastard and prick. May he always stay wretched." She took a sip then set her cup down. "So, have you hired a lawyer, or are you here to get names and numbers?"

Lindsey laughed. "I've got a lawyer."

"Yes!" Savannah's bright red lips sparkled as she grinned and pumped her fists into the air. "I knew it!"

Lindsey held up her finger. "Though I'm not leaving just yet. But just so you know, his days of carousing and ruling the roost are over. He's been…neutered."

"Do tell." Savannah arched her manicured eyebrows. "I have to hear this. Come on, girl. Spill."

Lindsey laughed again, jubilant at her friend's support. "All in good time. Before I can go, I need to find a way to support myself."

"No." Savannah barked. "You don't. I can't tell you how many women stay because they're afraid of losing everything. If your lawyer can't get you some cash, we'll get you one that can. I'll even front you the money if you need it."

Each friend reached over and placed a hand on hers. "Me too," Polly said. "Whatever you need, honey."

Genie smiled, tender and loving. "We don't have much, but we do have a bit tucked away in savings. If it gets you out of the spot you're in, it's yours."

Lindsey set her free hand on top of the pile as tears pricked her eyes. Her heart almost exploded with the love she had for these women. "Thank you, dears. I can't tell you how much that means to me. It melts my heart that you're so willing to go out on a limb for me."

Polly nodded. "Of course we are. Now, let's see if we can find someone better to represent you, and we'll get this thing rolling."

Lindsey shook her head. "You're all generous to a fault, but it isn't necessary."

Savannah sat back and folded her arms. "This had better be really good, Linds, or I'll just head over to his office and pop myself a cheater and his slut girlfriend." She held open her purse revealing the small handgun inside. "Sure, I'll go away for a bit, but Stewart will be dead a lot longer than I'll be in jail. You'll probably still get the insurance money too."

Lindsey laughed. "Oh, darlin'. Okay first let me explain, and then you can decide if you want to put a bullet in his brain."

"Forget his brain." Savannah beamed, closing her purse. "I'll shoot his pecker off."

The four of them burst out laughing. Patrons from nearby tables glanced their way then went back to their muted conversations.

Lindsey took a sip of coffee. "Like I said I need a way to support myself, so I started a business."

Savannah jerked back. "You? Really? That's awesome! I'll take two of whatever you're selling."

The other ladies nodded.

Lindsey laughed again. "You guys are too much. I'm not selling anything per se. I've opened a handyman business. In fact, I've got several employees already." She reached into her purse and pulled out the black leather-bound binder, flipped it open, and spun it around on the table.

The three women gawked at the images from the little plastic windows. Each of the cards had the picture of a man, ranging between twenty-something and forty-something, his name, and a short list of his likes and interests.

Savannah smiled. "Well, you certainly have great taste in employees. I'm particularly fond of Leon here." She tapped the image of a dark-haired, gray-eyed, thirty-year-old. "He could come and adjust my pipes any day."

"New Man Handyman." Genie tried the name out and

smiled. "Yes, that works. I don't understand the bio though. Savannah's boyfriend likes musicals, cooking, and long walks. What's that got to do with fixing things?"

Lindsey took a deep breath. This was it. She'd find out right here if her new business would be a smashing success or an utter failure. "Because these guys don't pour cement or clean gutters, though, I suppose they would if you asked them to." She looked at each of her friends. "They're escorts."

The women around the table fell into a stunned silence.

Savannah gave her an appreciative smile. "Wow, girl, I'm impressed; you have some serious balls."

Polly sat up. "Hey, I think I saw this guy." She pointed to Dios' picture and studied the small image closer. "Yeah, he was flirting with a cashier down at the market." Polly laughed. "The girl was practically drooling on her register."

Lindsey rolled her eyes. "That would be Angel. Dios tried to venture out on his own and used her as his first learning experience. It didn't take long before he was calling me like a little boy lost in a department store looking for his mommy."

Polly shook her head. "He's gorgeous." She looked around and lowered her voice. "But an escort service here in the Cove?" She sat back.

Her friends glanced at each other. Genie and Polly gave Savannah the go-ahead nod.

Savannah brushed back a wisp of hair. "So…oh my, there is so much; where to start? You are bold and ballsy, and that's one of the things we love so much about you."

The other two nodded their heads in agreement.

"But…wow. Okay, let's start with your husband. He's a prick, a bastard, a cheater, and a liar, but I don't think he's going to sit by and let you run an escort service from your living room. He's going to bring the police in and shut you down."

Lindsey smiled, picked up her coffee, and took a sip.

"You know how I told you that I'd neutered Stewart. Well, I wasn't kidding." She went on to explain how she'd found out about paying Cindie under the table, harboring an illegal, her visit to the sheriff, and how she'd slipped the proof into Stewart's satchel. As she continued, her friends' eyes grew wider and wider.

Savannah started to giggle. "So he'd been carrying around the proof of everything he'd been doing in his briefcase? You made him bring his own evidence to your meeting?" Her giggles turned to laughter, and soon they all joined her.

Lindsey wiped tears from her eyes. "Really, I just didn't want to have to go upstairs to get it. It comes down to simple laziness."

This brought on a fresh wave of laughter. They received several glares from nearby customers. Lindsey didn't pay them any attention, continuing her tale. "So after he realized he was screwed, I presented him with a couple of documents I had drawn up by my lawyer."

Savannah brightened. "Divorce papers? Are you gonna take him for everything he's worth?"

Lindsey shook her head. "No, not yet. When I was doing my research, I discovered that even though Stewart talks a big game, his company is teetering on bankruptcy. I'm holding him by the short hairs for it, but hiring Cindie under the table was a really smart financial move. Not a legal one, but a smart one. We don't have much in savings, and there is very little value in the house. If I divorce him now, I'll get next to nothing."

Genie raised her hand. "Okay, I'll bite, what did you give him?"

When Lindsey had first met the shy pastor's wife, she'd assumed the worst—boring and lombotomized by a zealot of a husband. She'd sidestepped the woman for fear of being religiousized by the same surgeon who removed the brains of all "believers." But one day after the Sunday sermon, Lindsey had walked in while Genie cried over a large glass of the sacred wine. As the pastor's wife spilled the sad tale of her life, the two had bonded over shitty husbands and crappy marriages, forging a deep friendship.

Lindsey grinned. "I made him sign away all rights to my company. After we make it a success, he'll have no claim on it."

Savannah slumped in her seat. "So you're not leaving him?"

"For now, no." Lindsey shook her head. "A divorce right now would be devastating. But once I'm financially solvent, I'm kicking his ass out. One of the other things the lawyer did was help me get my name off Stewart's company. When that crashes and burns, I won't be associated with it in any way."

Pursing her lips, Savannah studied her. "He signed everything?"

Lindsey nodded. "He really had no choice."

Savannah tapped her teeth with a long red fingernail. "So, you need us to spread the word about your little enterprise. Help you drum up clients?"

Genie raised her hand again. "You're essentially running a prostitution ring. Like they talk about on TV…only with men. That's what it comes down to."

Lindsey shook her head and chuckled. "No. I'm not a pimp; I'm running a domestic escort service."

The pastor's wife frowned. "I don't understand what that even means."

Lindsey directed her gaze at her old friend. "It's simple. If you want a gentleman to come over and spend the afternoon with you, listen to you, cook for you, chat with you, or whatever you fancy, call us and we set it up. If something…more happens between you and your gentleman, well then that's between the two of you. But this isn't a sex service. It's an entertainment business with some of the best eye candy the town has to offer."

Savannah sighed. "I saw something about this on TV. Escort services are legal in California, but they are constantly getting busted because they're usually just fronts for prostitution rings. Plus, if it ever comes back that you started this…"

Lindsey rubbed the back of her neck, frustrated her friends kept focusing on the negatives. Without their support and encouragement, this venture would be as dead as the deer on the front of her family's Christmas card. "What? What could happen? I've already dealt with the sheriff. I have already bartered with someone, a little of our services for a little of theirs, to handle the taxes and business documents and all that. Stewart's completely out."

She tightened her fists as though to prevent this great endeavor from slipping through her fingers. "What else could go wrong? A big scandal? Seriously, you know me. Do you think I care a fig if the tongues of this little town blab about me more than they already do? It's not like I have a stellar reputation. What's one more interesting little tidbit?"

Silence descended on the little group once again.

Savannah leaned back. "Alright, I can see the opportunities here. There are a lot of possible bad outcomes though, not the least of which could be for your employees. Husbands can be violent when jealous."

Lindsey smiled wide and folded her hands on the table. "Ladies, why should they be jealous of a gay man working for a legitimate business?"

Polly jolted, sitting up straight. "Wait. What? Gay? I must have missed something. This is an entirely different business model than what I imagined. The only possible customers of such an operation that I know about are Owen and Norman, and they're together. I'm sure there are more, but are there enough to create a viable market? Maybe you should move this to San Francisco?"

Lindsey laughed at her friend's consternation. "When I first set this up, Stewart informed me that Dios, my first employee, is gay. He said my Peruvian dresses like an extra from *Grease* and that his accent is fake. As Genie pointed out, Leon likes cooking and musicals. I can only imagine what Stewart would have to say about him. Stewie claims to have a sixth sense about such things and is able to 'read' people. I'm sure that everyone else's husbands will feel secure knowing that their wives' needs are being satisfied by the queer. Maybe I should rename the business, Gay Man Handyman?"

Savannah covered her mouth to keep coffee from spraying across the table, swallowed, and burst out laughing. After a moment, Polly, Genie, and Lindsey joined her. The unconditional love and support of these women relieved Lindsey of the burden she'd been lugging around since beginning this endeavor.

As their smiles abated, her three friends quieted down, each lost in thought. Lindsey let them have their time to contemplate, hiding her party girl smile behind a housewife latte.

Genie, who'd been staring off into space, hadn't said much during most of the exchange. Slowly she leaned forward, a wicked little grin spreading across her thin lips. "Can I see the employees again?"

Savannah dropped her cup onto the saucer. Hot coffee splashed onto the obnoxious yellow flowered tablecloth. Polly covered her chest and let out a small squeak. Lindsey took her friend's hand and squeezed it before opening the book back up and sliding it across the table.

Polly sighed and shook her head as her gaze lingered on Genie. "This isn't really my thing, but I know a few potential clients that might be interested."

Savannah's eyes widened and then narrowed, a sinister little grin capturing her lips. "I'm with Genie. Mark has been too busy watching ESPN, drinking beer, and getting fat to pay attention to me. I wouldn't mind having a handsome gent come over and cook for me. Would he do it shirtless?"

Party Girl Lindsey laughed long and hard. "Yes, of course. Whatever you want." She'd always known she had the best friends in the world, but today confirmed it yet again.

As Polly gazed at the little slips of cardboard, her eyes widened and her jaw dropped open. "Um, what the hell?" She pointed to Dios' card.

Lindsey looked at the card then back at her friend. "What?"

Polly tapped the name on the card. "Emigdio Jesús Christo. Jesus Christ. You have Jesus working for you?"

Lindsey shrugged. "He's Peruvian. It's pronounced hey-suese, but yeah, I guess so."

Savannah's mouth formed a perfect O. "You are pimping out a man named after the son of God? Oh my shit, girl, you're going to Hell for sure."

Genie turned to Polly. "I speak Spanish, and his first name is pronounced Ey-meeth-dio. It means demigod." Her wicked little grin widened as amusement danced in her eyes. "That is *so* hot." Genie crossed her arms on the table and looked over the top of her glasses. "Please sign me up for a regular Wednesday session for one thirty. If Paul asks what I'm doing, I'll tell him I'm spending my special time with Jesus."

The other three women gawked at her for a heartbeat and then burst out laughing again. This time, several patrons of the little coffee shop moved to tables further away from the group

When the ruckus died down, Savannah high-fived Lindsey. "Like I said, you've got some balls, girl. Big, brass ones."

The last piece of the puzzle fell into place as Lindsey's friends began collaborating with one another on how best to promote her new venture. As lists of potential clients and marketing notes formed, her world and her destiny clicked into place. The party animal and the domestic diva smiled and, in unison, raised their martini glasses to salute the new queen, and Madam, of Alabaster Cove.

Acknowledgements

First and foremost, I'd like to say thank you to my readers. It means the world to me that you've spent some of your valuable time in my crazy little world.

To all my friends and family: This book has been many, many years in the making, and I'd be nowhere without your love and support.

To my editor, Anya: Thank you for pushing for more. You call me on my crap, tell me I'm wrong on my facts, point out my many woefully sad writing mistakes, and always keep it real. I can't tell you how much your frank opinions and evaluations have helped improve my writing and storytelling.

To my Ninja Girl: Erin, I am beyond grateful to you. Without you, this book and my writing would not be anywhere near what it is today. Your expertise, patience, and brilliance both as a storyteller and as a grammar nerd have taught me more than I never knew, I never knew. Because of your "passive voice," "this what?" "telling," "give me more's," and a million other Erinisms, this book has reached a potential I never dreamed.

You are my Ideal Reader; when I write, I hear your laughter, see your smile, and feel your emotions. This pushes me to be more than my potential.

Erin, you are my best friend, my lover, and, even better, you are my beautiful bride. You make my cloudy days sunny, the unbearable bearable, and have taught my soul to dance. I love you more than words could ever express. #Always

Lastly, I wish to thank the citizens of Alabaster Cove. Thank you for letting me base my books on your beautiful town. I'll try my best to honor it and give it the credit you all so rightfully deserve.

Readers, if want to learn more about Alabaster Cove, I highly recommend visiting www.AlabasterCove.net for information on their city and on vacation opportunities.

About the Author

Deek lives in a rainy pocket in the Pacific Northwest with his stunning YA author bride, Erin Rhew, and their writing assistant, a fat tabby named Trinity. They enjoy lingering in the mornings, and often late into the night, caught up in Erin's fantastic fantasy worlds of noble princes and knights and entwined in Deek's dark underworld of the FBI and drug lords.

He and Erin love to share books by reading aloud to one another. In addition, they enjoy spending time with friends, running, boxing, lifting weights, and exploring the little town they call home.

Thank you for reading *Birth of an American Gigolo*. You can follow Deek and all his Rhewminations at www. DeekRhewBooks.com.

Please don't forget to leave a review on Amazon or Goodreads.